Return of the
Grudstone Ghosts

Return of the Grudstone Ghosts

Arthur Slade

COTEAU BOOKS
WWW.COTEAUBOOKS.COM

This novel is a work of fiction. Names, characters, places, and incidents either are the product of the author's imagination or are used fictitiously. Any resemblance to actual persons, living or dead, is coincidental.

Edited by Robert Currie.
Cover painting by Dawn Pearcey.
Cover and book design by Duncan Campbell.
Printed and bound in Canada by Kromar Printing Limited, Winnipeg, Canada.

National Library of Canada Cataloguing in Publication Data

Slade, Arthur G. (Arthur Gregory)
Return of the Grudstone ghosts

(Canadian chills)
ISBN 1-55050-212-3

1. Moose Jaw (Sask.)–Juvenile fiction. I. Title. II. Series.
PS8587.L343R47 2002   jc813'.54   C2002-910910-8
PZ7.S628835Re 2002

10 9 8 7 6 5 4 3 2 1

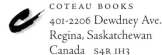

COTEAU BOOKS
401-2206 Dewdney Ave.
Regina, Saskatchewan
Canada   S4R 1H3

The publisher gratefully acknowledges the financial assistance of the Saskatchewan Arts Board, the Canada Council for the Arts, the Government of Canada through the Book Publishing Industry Development Program (BPIDP), and the City of Regina Arts Commission, for its publishing program.

*This book is dedicated to the memory
of my grandmother, Harriet Slade.*

CHAPTER ONE

OUT OF THE BELFRY

It all started with a long, fearful scream.

Well, not just any scream but the horrified shriek of my sixth grade teacher, Miss Angela Vindez. That screeching cry made me, Nick, and Peach look up from where we were sitting on the bench in front of St. Wolcott school. I was so shocked I dropped my notebook, and my pigtails stood on end.

The scream was followed by the sound of glass breaking far above us in the belfry, a tall old tower that cast a thin shadow across the school. Miss Vindez came shooting out a tiny window and plummeted towards us like a five-foot-two-inch sack of potatoes with flailing limbs.

She stopped suddenly in mid-air, then swung back

1

and forth like a pendulum, one arm pointing at the sky.

There was a thick rope circling her hand. It looked like someone had tried to lasso her. A split second later the rope snapped and she dropped out of sight onto the roof of the school.

The three of us – and half the student population – stood stunned and speechless.

"What's going on, Daphne?" Nick whispered, pushing his glasses to the top of his narrow nose. They slid down at once. The dimples in his cheeks were severely indented, which meant he was thinking hard. Nick and Peach always turned to me when things like this happened because I usually had an answer. But this time I just stared, my mouth open. *Catching flies*, as my Grandma Shea loved to say.

Men hollered in panic on the rooftop. This was followed by loud pounding footsteps. Then came a female scream that sounded like WILTHY KEECHER OV TARKNESS! There was a SMACK, and a man bellowed as if he'd been stung by a giant bee.

Even more students gathered around the school. We all gawked upwards until our necks ached.

"What's going on, Daphne?" This time it was Peach asking the question. We call her Peach because that's the colour of her hair – blonde with reddish tinges – and she has a dimpled chin that makes her look like a peach.

"What's going on?" she repeated. Maybe Peach thought I could see more because I was an inch taller than her and I wore glasses. I shrugged.

At that very moment sirens cut through the air and an ambulance peeled into the school yard, balancing on two tires. It slammed down, bounced, then screeched to a stop. Two tall men dashed out, holding a stretcher between them. The attendants were so thin they looked like upside-down exclamation marks with arms and legs.

A teacher held the school door open. The men zipped in and zipped back a minute later with Miss Vindez strapped to the stretcher. It was a good thing they had her belted tight or she would have bobbed right out.

I was lucky enough to be in the front of the crowd as they sped past. Miss Vindez's eyes were wide and white as eggs, her dark hair wild, her head whipping back and forth. And, as if that wasn't weird enough, she was hissing, "I ssssaw them out of the cornerssss of my eyessss. I ssssaw them. The grey creaturesss."

Then with a *thump thump* the ambulance doors slammed shut. The siren wailed, the back tires squealed and they were off, careening out of the parking lot and down to the Union Hospital. All of us school kids watched in wonder.

It was, after all, the first day of classes. My first day in grade seven. And if this was a sign of things to come it was going to be a very, verrrrry, long year.

"What's going on, Daphne?" Nick and Peach asked at the same time.

I frowned, pursed my lips. "I don't know," I answered, after a long dramatic pause, "but I'm gonna find out."

CHAPTER TWO

A ROSE BY ANY OTHER NAME

My name? Yes, I know. Daphne isn't the hippest name to have. You probably think my parents are cruel. That they sat around for hours thinking up names like *Gretchen* and *Winnifred* until finally they settled on *Daphne*. "It's perfect," they might have said, "it sounds like Daffy. She'll be teased for the rest of her life and will end up in the circus."

It didn't happen like that. They named me after my grandma, Daphne Shea. She's old and amazingly light on her feet, and she lived a life of crazy adventure before she retired here to Moose Jaw. She was trained as a spy at Camp X in Ontario, then was parachuted in to help the underground resistance in Paris during World War II. When the Nazis caught on, she made a daring escape on a fisherman's boat, landing in England. Which is where she met Grandpa. She gave birth to my father, climbed Mount Everest and biked across Canada. She said raising Dad was by far the hardest of those three things.

And she always has good advice. "Daphne," she once said when I was having a particularly bad day, "you've inherited your stocky body from me. You'll thank me for it as you get older. If you're thin as a stick, your coach will expect you to play basketball and excel! Excel! Excel! When you're in-between thin and thick no one knows how to take you or what you're supposed to do. So you can be full of surprises." That's my Grandma. Stuffed to the brim with good advice.

So you can probably guess...I love my name. It's old sounding and a little silly, and people always think because of my name and my glasses and my plain brown hair that I don't know what's going on. But I do. Just ask Peach and Nick, my two closest friends here in the Jaw. I'm pretty good at guessing things, and I've got a rep of being a Sherlock and a young scientist too.

And for getting into trouble.

Which was exactly what happened when I started looking into the Miss Vindez flying incident.

The next day at school there were more rumours winging around than there are pigeons in Crescent Park:

Miss Vindez had her heart broken and tried to end it all in a dramatic fall; she was mad, gone crazy from correcting too many exams with misspelled words; she had inhaled so much chalk dust, parts of her brain had shut down. Someone also said that after falling from that great height she sat up and decked Principal Peterka, who was coming over to see if she was alive. I dismissed all these tales as nothing but the ramblings of a bunch of grade seven students dizzy from excitement and light-headed from consuming too much sugar.

Sometimes my classmates mixed up video games and movies with real life.

I did find out that the shock of the fall had been too much for Miss Vindez and she'd slipped into a deep coma. I also learned the police had arrived at St. Wolcott, poked around the school for a while, and left an hour or two later. What had they found?

Nick approached me at recess. He's been my friend since grade four, and he's brilliant with math and science, but has never been much with colours: his socks were green, his pants light blue, his shirt yellow. He had the collar turned up as if he expected a thundershower inside the school. I'd told him to go undercover and dig for clues: he took his job very seriously.

Nick looked left, then right. "Got a tip for you, Daphne," he whispered in a deep, raspy voice. The opposite of his real voice. "See Bob. Over by the drinking fountain. The usual payment."

I nodded, but when I turned to say thanks, Nick was gone. Sniffing out another clue, I guessed.

I went to the drinking fountain. Bob Eckerweir, the janitor's son, was there smiling. He was a little pudgy, and he always wore his hat backwards. I guess no one ever told him which end should point to the front. His cheeks were dotted with freckles.

I slipped him a Snickers bar.

He snatched it from me, ripped the wrapping open and loudly munched on the bar, his mouth opening and closing like a huge power shovel at a construction site. A peanut escaped the destruction, dangled from his lip for a moment, then dived to freedom.

Detectives see some grisly sights. But I couldn't watch this display any longer. I opened my mouth to ask Bob a question – he put up his hand and made me wait.

Attitude. You get tonnes of it in my business. I call it being persnickety. And if there was one thing Bob was good at it was persnicketyness. I waited, tapping my foot. A loud smack announced he was finished. He wiped one side of his mouth with his sleeve.

I had been circling for far too long – I dove in like a F-15 fighter plane and strafed him with questions. "So what'd your dad say? Did he see anything? Was Miss

Vindez really crazy? What's the scoop? Tell me! Did she deck the principal?"

This inquisitive attack was a little bit too much for ol' Bob, who stepped back, wiped the other side of his mouth and gave me a look of disgust, as if I'd just asked him out on a date.

"Not. So. Fast." He paused. "I'll answer your questions." He paused again, picked between his teeth with a fingernail. "One by one." He finished his work, rubbed his nose with his right wrist. "Dad said he and Principal P were checking to see if Miss Vindez was okay, and when they got up to the school roof, she was wearing a noose and bibbling."

"Bibbling?" I echoed. Bob spoke a rather strange version of English. "Oh, babbling, you mean."

"*Babbling*...that's what I said! Miss Vindez's eyes were all googly, darting back and forth. Then Principal P came over and she sat up, pulled back her right arm, curled her fingers together and plowed him in the jaw, yelling, '*Filthy creature of darkness!*'"

"'*Filthy creature of darkness!*' Really?" So that's what she'd screamed from the top of the roof. I was writing all this down in my notebook. "Do you know why?"

"She was absolumly crazy."

"Absolutely, you mean?"

"That's what I said!" Bob stopped, crossed his arms.

"Do you want to hear or not?"

"Yes, yes, go on," I urged, but he stayed silent and I wondered if he wanted another Snickers bar. I was all out. I didn't even have a stick of gum. So I gave him my meanest, coldest stare, swearing I wouldn't blink first.

Sometimes you have to get a little pushy when you want info out of your stoolies.

Bob rolled his eyes and started up again. "So she called him filthy, and Dad said he had to hold her down and take the noose off her hand, and that's exactly what they did, and then the ambulance came and –"

"I think I know the rest," I interrupted. "Was there anything else weird? Think hard."

Bob narrowed his eyes. "Yeah, Dad said she smelled funny."

"What?" I could hear the rumours now, Miss Vindez jumped out of the belfry because her underarm deodorant had failed. "What kind of smell?"

"Well, like she'd been rolling in a bunch of flowers."

Intriguing.

"Why did she punch Principal Peterka?" I asked.

Bob shrugged. "I don't know. Guess she was deerlee-rious."

I didn't correct him. Instead, I stood drumming my foot, urging my mind into a higher gear. Something very important was missing. But what was it? If only I could think fast enough, I'd see it.

But I had my mental motor burning at full speed, and my mind wasn't jumping to any conclusions. Concussions, maybe, not conclusions. Desperate, I grabbed Bob by the shoulders and shook him. I'd seen this method work on TV. "Did she say anything else?" I practically shouted. I considered slapping him to jar his memory, or at least knock his hat in the right direction.

Bob concentrated for a second. He looked uncomfortable. He wasn't used to thinking hard. "Yeah," he answered a moment later, "she said, *Don't forget the pious, screaming children.*"

"Oh," which was all I could come up with, "Thanks." I let him go. Bob scowled at me, then turned and shuffled into the hallway, using his meaty fingers to brush off his shoulders where I had touched him.

Don't forget the pious, screaming children. Now what could that mean? Us, students? The St. Wolcott School choir? I would have to look up the word pious next time I was near a dictionary.

I let it all go and decided to visit the crime scene, the belfry, the room that housed the old, unused school bell (it had been replaced by an electronic buzzer and hadn't rung in living memory). Maybe there were a few clues waiting there that would unlock the secrets to this whole investigation.

You need two things to get to the belfry. A dependable pair of shoes and a crowbar to pry open the boarded up door marked: *No Admittance.* I had the shoes, but no crowbar. In order to get ahead one has to take a calculated risk – so I headed to the third floor, snuck down a deserted hallway, and when I came to the belfry door I discovered that all the boards had been removed. I was in luck!

Except there were two yellow strips of plastic that said: POLICE CRIME SCENE. DO NOT CROSS.

I pretended I couldn't read.

When I slowly pushed the door open, the hinges screeched like giant cave bats. I wormed my way inside and gently closed the door. The room smelled musty and old and smoky, as if no one had opened a window in about a hundred years. Ahead of me was a circular staircase that wound its way up into darkness.

I reached inside my backpack. I have a big long-handled flashlight that the Moose Jaw City Police gave me when I solved the riddle of the missing monkeys, back when I was in grade six. The flashlight has the inscription: *For the greatest detective in the world...Daphne Shea.* They were exaggerating a little. I'd settle for the greatest *grade seven* detective in the world.

Anyway, I lugged the flashlight out, clicked it on and began to pad upwards one step at a time, quiet as a cat.

I had no idea why Miss Vindez would want to go up there; as far as I knew no one ever climbed these stairs.

Like all the students of St. Wolcott, I'd heard the rumours about the ghosts. According to several imaginative sources, a group of spooks hung out in the belfry, filling out multiplication tables, doing lines and forever cleaning invisible chalkboards. Halloween night was the only time they could leave the tower and wander through the rest of the school. They would spend these few hours mixing up books inside students' lockers and teachers' desks.

I'd met a few ghosts in my time. Some friendly, others – well let's just say they put the bogey in bogeyman. But I wasn't sure if I believed these Wolcott ghost stories. I knew no spirits would be silly enough to spend their afterlife in a school.

Especially a school belfry in Moose Jaw, Saskatchewan.

A few strange things had happened up here. Last year a student said he heard voices and followed them up the stairs, only to fall through a step and sprain his ankle. The door had been barred and locked ever since.

When I got about halfway up the stairs, I saw that one of the steps was missing. I shone my flashlight down, lighting up the wooden floor below me. It was at least a seven metre fall, enough to break a bone or knock me out for a week and make me miss all my favorite TV shows. Maybe this was where that student fell from.

I took a deep breath and stretched my leg up to the next step, tested my footing, then slowly moved over the hole, gripping the banister in case the wood below my feet gave out.

I carried on without a backward glance. I was starting to feel a little worried, though. Each board creaked and cracked under my feet. How old were these stairs? Ninety-nine years? Two hundred? I knew St. Wolcott had been built on the site of an older school and that this tower and our cavernous library were all that was left of the previous building.

I couldn't imagine any reason why Miss Vindez would want to come up here.

I got to the top.

A thick wooden door led into the belfry. It was like something out of a dungeon, so heavy that a battering ram couldn't knock it down.

I tried to turn the giant rusty knob. It wouldn't budge. I pushed and the door creaked, but stayed still. I bent down and peeked through the keyhole.

It was black inside, except where a few thin shafts of light poked through the cracked walls. The old school bell hung somewhere high in the darkness, probably near the roof. White sheets covered desks and chairs, making eerie monstrous shapes. Past them was a chalkboard, a chest, piles of junk and something that looked like a gallows. I shivered.

Then I smelled a strange smell.

Something sweet.

I sniffed deeply, holding my nose close to the keyhole.

Flowers. It was like there was a garden inside. But what could possibly be the source of the scent? I squinted through the hole again. No vases stuffed with daffodils. Not even a rose.

But there was a shifting motion – a grey dark shape, moving back and forth. It disappeared behind the chalkboard. I stared, but nothing else appeared. Was it my imagination? Then came the sound of creaking boards. Someone was walking around on the other side of the door. Coming closer.

Suddenly it dawned on me – the noise wasn't inside the room. It was behind me. A chill ran down my spine.

"You are in the biggest trouble of your life," a deep voice muttered.

CHAPTER THREE

OL' BUG EYES

I screamed.

Then I spun, the flashlight held like a baton. I prepared to let loose a simultaneous *Keee-Yaaa!* and a karate kick that would make my sensei proud.

It was Principal Peterka. His oversized eyes stared down at me. They seemed to glow as if his brain was powered by nuclear fission. He had an elongated face that would only look normal in a carnival mirror. A white scar from his days as a hockey player cut a line through his right eyebrow.

"You're in serious trouble, Miss Shea. Why are you up here?"

"Uh." I paused and sucked in a deep breath, then wheezed out some air. Maybe he'd think I was having an asthma attack and take pity on me.

His eyes glared relentlessly. He put his hands on his hips.

"Uh," I repeated, hoping my brain would switch to supersonic-quick excuse mode. "Uh...I'm doing a piece for the St. Wolcott News on Miss Vindez's...accident. The inquiring minds of the school population have to know what really happened. They need the facts, sir. It's their democratic right."

"So you came up here without permission?"

Adults are very good at asking questions that are traps.

"I...uh...actually was looking for the washroom and took a wrong turn." I blinked a couple times and acted confused, holding my forehead with my hand as if I was about to faint. I wheezed out some more air. "It's only my second day in grade seven."

He loomed closer. His eyes grew even bigger: two luminescent death stars with pupils, powering up to shoot laser beams. "Do you expect me to believe that, Miss Shea?"

"No." I let my shoulders sag and stared at the floor. "I just want to make it the best piece for the paper that I can, Mr. Peterka."

"I applaud your hard work, but there are rules in St. Wolcott school, rules over seventy years old, and they are not to be broken. You will march yourself downstairs right this instant, Miss Shea, and you will not come back here again. EVER. Do you understand?"

"Yes, Mr. Peterka." I bowed my head and started shuffling down to the bottom floor of the belfry. He stayed one step behind me, like an oversized shadow, which freaked me out because the stairs were creaking so loud, I was sure one would break. I carefully crossed the broken stair. He followed, and we made it to the main floor without falling into oblivion.

Mr. Peterka closed the door to the belfry stairs, and with a CLICK it was locked. What was he hiding? I wondered. I guessed I wouldn't be heading back there any time soon.

"You can go now," he said, shooting me one more big-eyed, dirty look.

I slipped out of there, took the stairs to the main level and strode straight to my locker to pick up a few books for my class. The hallway was empty. When I went to spin the numbers on the combination lock, I found it was already open.

I pulled on the door.

A piece of paper fluttered out, circling to the floor like a wounded white moth. I bent down, picked it up and unfolded it.

Written in big red letters were the words: I KNOW

WHO DID IT! MEET ME BEHIND THE BRICK INCINER-
ATOR AT 4:15 TODAY.

I read it again. Who could have put this here? No
one else had my locker combination, except the school,
of course. Had someone looked over my shoulder? I
glanced around, then stopped myself. Whoever had left
the note was long gone. I tucked the paper into my jeans
and got ready for my next class.

The rest of the day went by quickly and I didn't find
out anything new, just heard the same old rumours
retold again and again. There was one new rumour –
that giant blood-sucking bats had attacked Miss
Vindez. I attributed this one to a Dracula movie that
was on TV last weekend. All of my teachers seemed rattled though, as if they hadn't slept the night before.

Then, just as I was leaving class, a voice whispered,
"Miss Vindez is out of her coma. Heard it by the coffee
machine."

I turned, but Nick was already gone, just another
head in a throng of grade seveners.

This was good news. My bet was that she could
answer a few of my questions, assuming her brains
weren't entirely scrambled.

Finally the bell rang. I hung around for a few minutes, and didn't head towards the back doors until most
of my fellow students were gone. On my way I passed

Principal Peterka. His arms were crossed. He glared at me with his satellite-sized eyes.

Did he know what I was doing?

Was he going to stop me?

I kept walking. It wasn't until I had opened the back door that I dared to sneak a glance behind me.

He was gone. He had probably disappeared into the staff room. Grinning as he wrote up his list of students on detention.

I marched out into the school yard, wanting to get to the bottom of this mysterious note as soon as possible. I went past the baseball diamond and the track and made a beeline towards the big, brick incinerator. I knew the school didn't use it anymore; all the trash was stored in metal dumpsters and hauled away in garbage trucks. But years ago they burned all their junk here...test papers, stage sets, broken baseball bats, old chalk brushes, anything you could imagine.

I looked over my shoulder. There was no one to be seen; the school seemed deserted. I glanced up at the belfry, perhaps one of the oldest structures in Moose Jaw.

Something moved across the broken window.

My heart stopped. I stared.

Again something flapped its way into sight, and disappeared.

It was a curtain. It had to be, but it didn't appear

again. I turned back towards the incinerator.

It took me a moment to get my legs working.

I came closer, touched the rough blocks. I smelled the faintest scent of ashes.

This is stupid, Daphne, I thought to myself. You have no idea who you're dealing with out here. It could be the same person who pushed Miss Vindez out the window.

If anyone had.

I thought briefly about turning back. Just calling it a day.

Then I remembered something my grandma always says to me whenever I get scared: *Are ya chicken, Daphne? Get plucky or you'll be plucked!*

I went around the corner of the incinerator.

CHAPTER FOUR

GREY SHADOWS IN THE DARKNESS

"*Heluzzzlebuzzle eee! Heluzzzlebuzzle eeee!*"

There was a middle-aged, balding man rolling on the ground, mumbling in distress. His hands were bound with hockey stick tape, and he was gagged with a giant dotted blue handkerchief.

"*Luzzzle eee!*" he cried, turning towards me, his eyes wide. I recognized him. He was St. Wolcott's janitor: Mr. Eckerweir. The father of Bob, the Snickers boy.

"Are you okay?" I asked.

His eyes rolled around in their sockets, then looked down at his hands. "*Luzzzle eee!*" he repeated. Was he speaking Chinese?

"Oh," I said. Finally it was dawning on me. "*Loosen me...help, loosen me.* Is that what you're saying?"

Mr. Eckerweir nodded quickly.

I leaned over, grabbed at the tape around his hands, and began tearing away like it was Christmas morning. It took a few seconds of work; then with a superhuman yank that I usually reserve for pull-starting the lawn mower, I ripped the last of the tape from his arms.

"HAAA-OWWW!"

I loosened his gag. "What?"

"Ow! You yanked half the hair from my arms. I'll freeze to death this winter."

"Oh...sorry, Mr. Eckerweir." I dropped the ball of tape I had gathered. "I don't always know my own strength."

"It's all right. Thank you...thank you for saving me, Miss Shoe."

"It's Shea, actually. Daphne Shea."

"Oh. Sorry." He felt his head. "I'm a little fraggled."

Like father, like son, I thought. "Frazzled, you mean?"

"No. Definitely fraggled. My thoughts seem to be...fragmented." He latched onto the incinerator wall and dragged himself to his feet. Mr. Eckerweir was a smidgen taller than me, with a stomach so round it looked like he'd swallowed a bowling ball. He started brushing dust off his chest. What little hair he did have on his head was poking out the sides of his skull like porcupine quills.

"Who did this to you?" I asked.

He blinked. It took him a moment to answer. "It all happened so fast. It's confusing. I was waiting here and then –" he started to breathe quickly in and out "– then the grey shadows, were reaching, reaching –" his eyes widened "– with long thick arms, stretching like tentacles out of the incinerator and grabbing me by the neck, by the legs and then..." He was holding his breath now, his face red as a robin's chest. He let out a big blast of air that parted my hair. "...I was like you found me."

"Did you know these people?"

Mr. Eckerweir was holding his head now, as if I had asked him which year Columbus sailed the ocean blue. "I...I...don't think they were people."

"What?"

He squeezed his temples with both hands, trying to squish in his thoughts, I supposed. "They were grey...the grey things...maybe they were people, maybe not...one was big and tall, but misty."

I remembered what Miss Vindez had shouted before being loaded into the ambulance: *I ssssaw them out of the cornerssss of my eyessss. I ssssaw them. The grey creaturesss.*

Were these the same grey creatures?

"They grabbed you, did they? So they *were* real then. They had a solid form."

He seemed lost for a moment, then raised a finger and exclaimed, "Yes! They grabbed me. They did and they said: *Don't speak a word of this!*"

"Speak a word of what?"

He shrugged. "That's the problem. I don't know."

He was still confused, so I decided to switch topics. "Did you put the note in my locker?" It only made sense; the janitor would know everyone's locker numbers.

"Note?" Mr. Eckerweir stared into space. "Locker?" He paused. "Yes," he said quietly. "Yes!" He pointed his finger to the sky again. "I knew you were investigating the terrible incident involving Miss Vindez. My son told me. So I wanted to tell you that..."

"That what?"

"I...I don't seem to remember. I was to warn you, about something...someone bad in the school. Yes!" he declared, "Someone bad is in the school! They're possessed!"

"Who? One of the teachers? Is it Mr. Widdles, the gym instructor? Is that why he makes us run so many laps? I knew it! Never trust anyone who says, 'No pain, no gain,' then laughs."

Mr. Eckerweir shook his head. "I...I don't know. It's all so confusing. There's a big grey storm cloud in my head." He leaned against the incinerator. "That's all I can tell you now. I should go finish my work. There's floors to mop, toilets to clean, brushes to wash. Got to check the furnace, too. I'm the janitor."

"Will you be all right? Do you need help to walk?"

"No. Uh. I'm fine." He didn't sound too sure of himself. "I just have to get back to the school."

He stumbled towards the wire fence that surrounded St. Wolcott. "Uh…Mr. Eckerweir. The school's the other way."

He nodded, smiled, then made a big circle and headed in the direction of the gym. I watched him wobble and stagger to the doors and disappear inside.

Possessed? Someone was possessed here? That sounded a little out of my league. I was never comfortable with black magic and witchcraft and all those other eerie things. They always had something to do with hanging around shadowy places at midnight when I'd rather be safe and toasty warm in my bed.

My cousin Wally was much better for that stuff. But he was far, far away in Winnipeg, and I didn't make enough money from my allowance to fly him out here.

So I would have to do my best with what I had.

I took a moment to snoop around the incinerator, in case whoever – whatever – had tied up Mr. Eckerweir had left some sort of clue.

But I saw nothing, no footprints, no matchbooks, not even a sign of a struggle. I grabbed the metal door of the incinerator, and pulled it open. It made a creaking rusty spring sound that reminded me of someone dragging fingernails across a chalkboard.

I peered inside. There were still grey ashes in thick piles. I smelled the old aroma of burnt paper and textbooks.

There was also a roll of tape.

I grabbed it and let the door go. It slammed shut like a metal mouth.

I examined my prize. It was hockey tape. The same kind that had been used on Mr. Eckerweir. They had taped him up, then thrown the tape in there.

Things were just getting weirder and weirder.

I looked back at the belfry. It was ugly and ominous – same as it always was – but nothing moved in the broken window. Not at the moment, anyway.

I knew there was only one thing I could do.

CHAPTER FIVE

THE QUIET ROOM

A few seconds later I was inside the school. The halls were empty, as if a big wind had blasted through and swept all the students away. My runners squeaked on the floor and I made a note to myself to ask Mom and Dad to buy squeakless shoes once I outgrew these.

I stopped in the girls' washroom, stood tippy-toe on the toilet in the stall against the far wall and opened the window a few centimetres. Then I left.

I squeaked down the hall, trotting by row after row of lockers, past the entrance to the gymnasium – or gym-nausea as my friend, Peach, called it – and stopped at the door marked with that mysterious, magical three-syllable word: *Library*.

If you asked *how do I get to the library?* a lot of my fellow students wouldn't know where to point or even what the word meant. They might say it's over that way or up there, or mumble that it's near the lunch room. Others would just shrug.

I spend a lot of my time inside this quiet room. It's the only area in the whole school where teachers can't yell at you, because everyone's required to whisper. It's also one of the best hiding places if you need to avoid the local bully or some other annoying person.

And, of course, it's a room full of books.

And books have words, and words explain things.

And being a detective, I like to have an explanation for everything.

I slipped through the door. Miss Kravitz glanced up at me. "Hi, Daphne," she whispered. She wasn't your usual librarian. She was old, yes, maybe twenty-two or three, but she always wore bright clothes, and despite spending all her time reading and filing books, she didn't wear glasses. In fact, she was almost hip. Her hair was short and her face narrow and pleasant.

She pulled an earphone out of her ear and set it next to her Walkman. *The Bare Naked Ladies* sang a song about having a million dollars.

"You're studying kind of late," Miss Kravitz said. "Is there something I can help you find?"

I nodded. "I want to know everything there is about

the school that was built before St. Wolcott."

Miss Kravitz smiled. "That's easy. Row C, in the 700s. Get the big old book called *The Tunnels and Tribulations of Moose Jaw*. It'll tell you everything you want to know and more. A lot more."

I followed her directions, went down Row C and searched around. I squinted at the different titles: *Moose Jaw Memories, All Roads Lead to Moose Jaw, Bingo! Fun and Games in the Jaw,* and a variety of other titles that hadn't been touched for years. Right at the bottom, I discovered the book Miss Kravitz had suggested. It was about three times as thick as a dictionary. I leaned down and heaved, grunting out loud, and feeling like one of those Olympic power-lifters. I struggled to get it up to chest level, then, suddenly top heavy, staggered over to the nearest table. I reached my destination and dropped the massive tome with a bang, testing the table's legs.

Oh, I should explain that *tome* is one of those words that I like to say every once in a while. It means "big, old book" as far as I know. Try it in a sentence sometime, like, "Would you mind carrying my tomes for me?"

You get the strangest looks.

Like I said, when I dropped the tome it made a loud cannon-like bang. I glanced at Miss Kravitz, but she was busy filling out forms and bopping her head to the beat, her headphones jammed back into her ears. I pulled out a chair and blew dust off the cover. A grey cloud drifted over the table and down to the floor.

Then I attempted to open *The Tunnels and Tribulations of Moose Jaw*. Easier said than done – an army of spiders had used their webs to tie it closed forever. Yuck! With a huge tug I snapped the white sticky strands and pried the covers open, then quickly wiped my hands on my pants.

Inside was the complete story of Moose Jaw: from the ice age to the nineteen seventies. The book explained that the city was named after a creek in the shape of a Moose's jaw. That made perfect sense, there are so many winding creeks around here. I read a bit further. It turns out that a man used a moose's jaw to fix his wagon wheel – and so he called the spot Moose Jaw. What was the real story? Nobody seemed to know.

I quickly skipped ahead, read a little about the Canadian Pacific Railroad coming through, and settled on the 1920s: Moose Jaw's gangster years.

Or as Nick would say: *the gangsta years.*

There was a piece on the boom in the population and how an event called prohibition drew a number of criminals to our lovely town. This led people to nickname the place "Little Chicago." A few paragraphs were dedicated to Al Capone, a famous crook from Chicago, who controlled bookie joints, gambling houses, race tracks, nightclubs, and breweries and made $100,000,000 a year while doing it. He was sometimes called Scarface because of scars he got from a fight in a bar. But even all his money and power didn't keep him safe. So he would take a trip to Moose Jaw whenever things were too hot in the real Chicago. By too hot they didn't mean temperature; they meant the police – the heat – made it too hot for him to do his work.

Al's main rival was a hawk-nosed, mean-tempered man named Iron Fist Ivan. He'd lost his hand in a tommy gun shoot out, so he replaced it with an iron fist. He used that fist to smash his way into the underworld, crushing his enemies and anything that got in his way. He and Capone were always butting heads. But even Iron Fist Ivan needed a holiday once in awhile – so he'd slip up to the Jaw for a rest.

It was during those days that the tunnels were built under the city, making it look like a giant ant nest.

I turned the page and my heart stopped.

There was a picture of a place called Grudstone School.

It was exactly where St. Wolcott school now sat. The belfry towered above a twisting, tall, brick building with narrow windows, a building that looked more like a prison than a place to educate kids. Children were out-side in rows, posing for class pictures.

There was something frightening about the black and white photograph. It was grainy and blurry, as if it had been a gloomy, foggy day. The student's uniforms were grey, their faces were grey, and their eyes were dull and tired. It looked like no one had slept for weeks before they took this photo.

It just seemed to have *bad news* written all over it.

I read below the picture:

Grudstone school was built in the late 1800s by million-aire Charles Grudstone, who had the bell in the belfry especially shipped in from an old German Church. On the final day of construction Mr. Grudstone helped place the last brick, then suffered a massive heart attack and died right on the spot. The school operated for the next 27 years, though it gained the reputation of being a home to misfortune. School drama performances were often stricken with bizarre collapses of sets or sudden black-outs. The sewer backed up and several teachers became sick from the smell and never returned. One parent slipped on the front stairs, rolled all the way down and broke his back. This is the final picture of Grudstone School, taken in 1927, three days before the building mysteriously caught fire and burned to the ground. Twelve students and one unidentified man passed away in the blaze. The school was demolished, except for the belfry and the library, the only standing structures not permanently damaged by the fire. It is now the site of St. Wolcott school.

Well, it's always nice to find out that your school is a home to the biggest blot of bad luck this side of Regina.

I examined the picture again, flipped ahead in the book, but I couldn't find anything else about Grudstone.

I wondered who had started the fire and who the mysterious, unidentified man could be.

Had he just wandered into the school by accident?

Or was he somehow involved?

I would probably never know. All this had happened over seventy years ago. But the bad luck was still winging its way around our school, searching for someone to land on.

And that someone was Miss Vindez.

CHAPTER SIX

ABOUT THIS HIGH DIVE ACT OF YOURS

"Miss Vindez," I whispered. I gently touched her shoulder. "Miss Vindez."

No answer.

It was 7:45 p.m. I was on the fourth floor of the Union Hospital.

How did I get here when the only people who were allowed to visit Miss Vindez were next of kin? It wasn't easy. I couldn't fool anyone into thinking I was part of her family: she was tanned; my skin was white as toothpaste. She had thick, curly black hair; mine was brown and thin and straight. Her eyes were tiny, dark and worldly; mine floated behind my thick glasses like two green fish.

You get the picture.

So I marched right through the front doors of the hospital, walked straight into the first office I saw and announced to the surprised woman sitting behind a desk: "I want to be a doctor just like you, Doctor Davern."

I had, of course, taken the time to read her name on the door before I pushed my way in.

Doctor Claire Davern stared up at me for a long moment. Her face was thin and long and probably spent most of its time being crabby. I wasn't sure if she was going to yell at me or not. Then a smile creaked its way across her lips, and she stood up and said: "What a bright career choice for a bright young girl." She showed me around the hospital, briefly, because she was very, very busy: doctors are always busy, just ask the next one you see. Then she patted my shoulder, sighed, and handed me off to one of the nurses at the nurse's station.

While I chatted with Nurse Wilkins, telling her how much I wanted to grow up and become a nurse, a little alarm sounded on the wall. She left me alone in the station and I found Miss Vindez's room number on the computer.

Nurse Wilkins wobbled back a minute later, saying, "That's what a nurse's life is all about. Do this, get this, don't forget the orange juice." It turned out the emergency was one of the patients wanting something to drink. I told her how brave she was and quickly excused myself, pretending to leave the building. But instead of descending to the main exit, I paused on the stairs until the coast was clear and snuck down the hall to Miss Vindez's room.

I spent the next five minutes standing beside Miss Vindez, whispering her name and attempting to awaken her. Any second now a nurse could come by to check on her, see me, scream, and call the cops.

Or at least toss me out on my ear.

I poked my sixth grade teacher's shoulder again. "Miss Vindez!" Still nothing. I switched tactics. "Miss Vindez, the school's on fire!"

Her big eyes shot open. "Fire!" she whispered, her voice all gravelly. "Single file, everyone! Single file!" She gawked around, saw me. "Single file, Daphne!"

"It's okay, Miss Vindez. There's no fire. And we're not at school now."

"Well, you have your backpack on." She pointed with a shaky finger.

"I always wear it. I just said there was a fire to wake you."

"Do you have your homework done?"

"I...uh...I'm in grade seven, now," I said. This wasn't

how I wanted things to go. "I'm not in your class."

"Just because you're not in my class anymore doesn't mean you shouldn't do your homework. You know better than that, Daphne."

"I'm doing it right now," I whispered, desperately.

"What do you mean?"

I paused. "I'm doing a paper. On a thing that happened at the school. I...I want to ask you about your accident."

"Accident?" She sounded alarmed. "I was in an accident?"

"Yes. You fell out a window in the belfry. Do you remember?"

Miss Vindez went pale. She grabbed my hand and squeezed it so tightly that I thought my fingers would stay bent at odd angles for the rest of my life.

"I! Remember!" she shouted. "Yes! Now, I remember! The falling, that feeling of being weightless, the rope around my arm, the roof of the school coming up big, black and fast. The –"

"Uh...Miss Vindez?"

"Yes?" She blinked about five times in a row.

"Please let go of my hand."

She did so and I shook it out, massaging my fingers with my left hand, making sure all of them still worked. They did, though I might have trouble holding a pencil or making shadow puppets.

I turned back to her. "Tell me what you remember. Please."

Miss Vindez stared me right in the eye. "Did you ever think I was batty, Daphne?" she asked seriously.

"Uh...no."

"I'm too young to be batty, right? I'm only thirty-five. Far too young to be batty."

Thirty-five sounded old enough to be batty to me, but that's not what I told her. "You're not batty, Miss Vindez. You're cool." And she was. She had always been my favorite teacher, full of spunk and ready to forgive us if the dog had somehow eaten our assignments three times in a row.

By the way, our family doesn't own a dog. Just a parrot named Diefenbaker.

Miss Vindez was silent for a moment. "But I saw things that made me think I was batty. Up in the belfry." She paused. "Batty in the belfry...that's kind of funny, isn't it?" She smiled, then frowned. "Except it wasn't funny...I heard voices so I went up there." She pointed at the ceiling; maybe she thought she was still in the school. "There were lots of voices. I thought they were students, but they weren't. They were scary things. Bad things. Grey and shifting and smelling like flowers, and singing. Singing. That's what they did, they sang."

"What were they?"

She kept talking, as if she hadn't heard me. "They were like children – pious screaming children."

I swallowed. She'd said the same thing when they took her out of the school.

"They sang, but screamed too. I backed away, but they surrounded me. I couldn't even yell for help, I was so frightened. A shadowy shape drifted towards me and sang in a falsetto, 'He's coming, he's here, the bad man bringing fear.' And I whispered, 'What bad man?' Another voice echoed in a booming tenor, 'Watch out, watch out, he's unholy blessed, he's a filthy creature of darkness.'"

I shuddered. Who could the creature be?

"Then the door to the belfry swung open and this blur flew towards me, its big hands reaching out of the darkness. It was a black shadow and it looked like a man, but it was moving too fast to tell for sure. It came right through the circle of grey shapes as if they weren't even there.

"I jumped back. Then I was tripping over a box and a snake curled around my neck."

"A snake? A boa constrictor?"

"No. I thought it was a snake and I yanked it off. It was a noose, the man-thing had somehow slipped it over me. The noose tightened around my hand and I was caught. *Beware, beware,* the small creatures screamed and sang at the same time. Then for one moment I could see them all clearly, children in old school uniforms. But what were they doing up there? I was pushed or I fell – I don't know what happened next. All I know is there was glass shattering and then I was falling, falling, the roof of the school coming up big, black and fast, the sound of the pious singing children still in my ears." She stopped, closed her eyes and took in a deep breath.

"And then you hit the roof."

"Yes. I hit it hard."

"And you punched Principal Peterka."

She stared right at me. Her face pinched together, pale and frightened. "No...not him. No, I was hitting the bad man. The filthy creature of darkness. I was hitting him." She sat up suddenly and shrieked, "He's here! He's here!" then collapsed on her bed, out like a light. I gawked around; there was no one else in the room.

"Miss Vindez," I whispered. I listened; she was still breathing. I touched the side of her neck, felt for her heartbeat. She was alive, at least. The power of the memory must have been too much for her brain.

But I wanted to be sure she was fine. I pressed the buzzer that summoned the nurse, then snuck out of the room, and down the back stairs.

A moment later I was standing outside the hospital, wondering which way I should go.

CHAPTER SEVEN

ON THE MAP

My grandfather always used to say, "When there are two paths in the road and you don't know where to go, drive right between them, and blow up anything that gets in your way."

He was a tank commander in World War II, so I guess he knew what he was talking about. Though apparently he wasn't the best driver in the world. Grandma said he spent most of his time getting stuck in mud.

I do wish he'd explained everything a bit more clearly. As far as I could see, I had two choices: go home and call it quits for the night, or keep looking for clues.

I couldn't make up my mind.

And I couldn't drive between the two choices. Or could I?

My feet led me away from the hospital. While I walked, my brain sifted through everything that I already knew, trying to find a nugget of gold.

Miss Vindez had fallen out the window after being chased by grey figures that she said might be children. They had warned her of a filthy creature of darkness. The janitor, Mr. Eckerweir, had been tied up by grey people, and had told me that someone in the school was possessed. The school was built on the site of an older school called Grudstone, where people had died. The whole place was jammed full of bad luck.

My best option was to trot right home, retreat to my bed, and in the morning ask Mom and Dad to transfer me to a new school.

Preferably one without a belfry.

But that wasn't the Daphne way of doing things. No, I had always believed in sticking it out to the very end. Digging until I hit bottom. Never retreat, never surrender!

Yes, I'm hard-headed. It comes in handy when you want to be a detective.

For a brief instant I thought of gingersnap cookies. Only for a microsecond, but it was enough to make me salivate. My feet automatically took me to my grandma's house, a tall, three-storey brick and wood castle with giant French doors. It's right across from Crescent Park.

And it always feels a little emptier since Grandpa passed away.

I walked up and pressed the bell. Grandma Shea came to the door, dressed in a track suit. She was wearing runners and had her long, grey hair tied back. "We've been expecting you," she said.

"We?" I asked.

She opened the door and motioned for me to enter. I did so.

Nick and Peach were kneeling on the living-room floor, examining a mess of maps. They both glanced up.

"You're here!" Nick exclaimed. He pushed his glasses against his nose and squinted at me. He was dressed all in black now, except for a pair of yellow socks. "It's about time. We searched all over for you."

"What are you doing here?" I asked.

"What do you think?" He huffed. "I've been digging around for clues at city hall, going so deep undercover that I didn't even remember who I was." He stopped, waiting for someone to laugh, but no one did. "Well, anyway," he said, frostily, "we stopped by your house to show you these, but you weren't home. So we came to your grandma's."

"How'd you know I'd show up here?" I asked.

"I told them you would," Grandma said, "because I baked gingersnap cookies. And you always come over when I do that."

"I...I..." A plate of gingersnap cookies was sitting on the end table. Grandma was right. Somehow, I had thought of gingersnaps even tonight. Was I psychic? If that was the case then I didn't know helpful things like exactly when the teacher would give a pop quiz, what stocks to invest in or which game the Moose Jaw Warriors would win. I only knew when Grandma Shea baked gingersnaps.

I guess it's better than no ESP at all.

"You should take a gander at what your friends have discovered," Grandma suggested, shoving the plate of cookies a few centimetres from my nose. I took a snap, bit down on it. Still warm and moist with just enough ginger to make your taste buds say "yum!" Exactly how I liked it.

"Come on." Peach motioned to me. "This is just so incredibly, amazingly interesting."

I walked over, knelt down on the hardwood floor. One of the maps was an old blueprint that had been torn into pieces. Nick and Peach had taped it back together.

I stared. It was the blueprint of a building. The date on the bottom said 1899. I squinted, saw an outline of a tower, and a main structure the size of a fortress. "This is Grudstone School."

"Yes!" Nick said, "It's the school that was built before St. Wolcott by –"

"Charles Grudstone," I finished for him. Nick

gawked at me like I'd sprouted a second head. "I read about it earlier today," I explained, "all about the fire."

"So you know that," Peach said, sounding a little disappointed that she wasn't one step ahead of me. She bit into a gingersnap and chewed thoughtfully. "We should have guessed. But Nick found something you may not know about."

"What?" I asked.

Nick smiled. "Look at this." He pointed at another old map. It was criss-crossed with streets and rectangles that I thought must be buildings. There were names on the streets. I squinted, getting closer. It was like a map of downtown Moose Jaw, but different. Then it dawned on me. "These are the underground tunnels from the old days."

Nick nodded. "Yes. They run through the downtown area and all over the place. It's funny the whole town doesn't just collapse. But look." He pointed at a long, narrow tunnel that headed away from Main Street. "See!" He followed it on the map. "It ends up at Grudstone School."

"What?" I peered closer, saw where his pencil-thin finger was tracing the tunnel. "It does, doesn't it? In fact, it looks like –"

"It's right under the belfry tower," Peach finished for me. "If you examine the Grudstone school blueprints

49

you can see that. Isn't it cool?"

It *was* cool, I thought. "This must be even older than the other tunnels. Most of them were built in the early 1900's...I think. I wonder what it was for."

Nick pushed up his glasses again. "Who knows? The gangsters probably used it though. At least it was on this map."

"Do you think it's still there?"

"I bet it is," Nick said. "They were all pretty sturdy tunnels. Many were built by the Chinese. And if there's one group of people who know how to build things, it's the Chinese. Why just look at The Great Wall of China. Now construction was started in the seventh century BC –"

"Wait!" I formed a T with my hands, signaling a time out. Once Nick got going on any topic he was impossible to stop. "You can give us the lecture on the Great Wall later...on all of China if you want. Right now I have some stuff I think you guys should hear."

Nick seemed a little hurt that I'd cut him off. He grabbed a gingersnap and sulkily chewed it. Once I started talking his look changed for the better, and I knew I had both his and Peach's total attention. Grandma leaned ahead, too – her computer-like brain taking in every word and analyzing the situation. I told them about finding the janitor bound and gagged, and all about Miss Vindez and her grey shadows in the belfry. When I finished, they stared at me in silence.

"Well?" I asked. "What do you think? What's going on in those heads of yours? Is it ghosts?"

"Ghosts! Possessions!" Nick practically spit out the words and half his cookie. I leaned away from him, knowing what was coming next. "You know there's no scientific data at all to support the existence of ghosts. Why back in 1954 when the FBI did the famous Red Book examination of –"

"I didn't say *I* thought there were ghosts," I interrupted again. "That's what it sounded like to Miss Vindez. That's all. I'm not sure what's going on."

"You do know that Draco is culminating," Grandma said.

"Excuse me?" I said. "Who's Draco?"

"And what's he cultivating?" Peach asked.

Grandma shook her head, like we'd made a rookie mistake. "It's not a who, it's a what. Draco – the dragon constellation – is at its highest point tonight." She paused. "It's either completely irrelevant, or it affects everything."

"Draco," Nick said. "Now why didn't I think of that? The position of the moon and constellations can have some bearing on human behaviour. There was a study in 1987..." He glanced over, saw the look of consternation in my eyes. "Uh, which I'll tell you all about some other day."

"How could a constellation cause all these freaky things at the school?" I asked.

Grandma shrugged. "I don't know. My brain has slowed down since retirement. I do find the events at your school a little worrying. Keep digging for information, but don't go doing anything crazy without telling me. Okay?" We nodded. She got up. "Well, I'm going for my power walk. You three should probably head for home. The best way to solve a mystery is to have a good night's sleep." She headed out the door, leaving us staring after her.

"There's definitely a lot of bad karma floating around our school and it's not even exam time," Peach said. "What are we going to do?"

I took a moment to think. I wasn't sure if they would like my plan, so I decided to run what I was going to say through my head a few times. I wanted to give them a speech so full of motivation that they couldn't, wouldn't ever say no.

"We have to break into the school," I blurted.

"What!" Nick exclaimed. "That's completely illegal! We'd be expelled."

"Not if we don't get caught," I countered.

"Your grandma told us not to do anything crazy."

"She's just being protective. We're professionals. We'll go in and get out quick."

"Why do you want us to do this, Daphne?" Peach asked, calmly. "You must have a good reason."

"Because, as far as I can figure out, everything that's going weird in our school, from Miss Vindez flying out a window to the janitor being tied up, has something to do with the belfry."

"So you want us to break into the school and climb up to the belfry?" Nick asked.

"Yeah, that's my plan. I don't know what was up there, but I have to find out, and I can't without your help. I was at the top of the belfry stairs this morning but couldn't get in – Mr. Peterka stopped me. I did get a chance to look in the key hole, and I saw something moving in there. I don't know what it could have been. Just thinking about it kinda freaks me out. But I have to go look for myself."

"Why do you need us?" Nick asked.

"Because we're a team," I shot back. "And because you'll have to give me a boost into the girl's bathroom. I left the window open."

I stared at them both, trying to read their thoughts. All I got was an image of gingersnaps. Peach and Nick stared back, their faces stern. Weren't they going to come? We always did these things together. I had to do something.

In desperation I stuck out my hand, palm down, like

we were a basketball team and just about to start a game. "Are you in?" I asked.

They were silent for a second, then Peach and Nick put their hands on top of mine and said, "We're in. Let's go."

A moment later I had the maps all folded carefully and hidden in my backpack.

CHAPTER EIGHT

CLICK! CLICK!

It was one of those clear, perfectly still nights. Not even the slightest wisp of a wind. I couldn't help but think this was the calm before the storm. As we trotted through Crescent Park, we crossed a grassy knoll where there were no street lights around and we could actually see the stars.

"Hey!" Nick yelled suddenly.

Peach and I turned around. He was standing behind us, staring straight up.

"Hey! What?" I yelled back. "What do you see?"

"Your grandma was right!" He put his hands around his eyes as if he were looking through a pair of imaginary binoculars. "Draco is at its highest point in the sky. It's just blazing away up there. I didn't think it was till later in the year."

Something about all this gave me the shivers. The Dragon constellation was at its highest point. That could only mean bad news for us. "Where is it?" I asked.

Nick pointed. "Right next to the Big Dipper. See those four stars...that's Draco's head. And the tail loops around the Big and Little Dippers."

I found the Big Dipper, followed Nick's directions. I saw the shape of a dragon. It seemed to be burning in the sky, bright as the lights on a fire truck.

"It should be in perfect position later tonight – just after midnight, I bet," Nick said.

My stomach turned over. My heart skipped a beat.

"Let's go," I commanded.

"But I haven't seen it yet," Peach said.

"I'm sorry. But we have to go. Now." I started walking towards the school. I was getting a really bad feeling about all of this. *Way bad*, as some of my cooler friends would say.

"What's the hurry?" Peach asked. She and Nick were a step behind me.

"I don't know," I said, admitting the truth. "I just have this feeling that a lot of things are going to happen tonight. And we better be there to see them. Or stop them."

We silently walked the next few blocks until we

caught sight of St. Wolcott. It seemed it had grown in the last few hours; it loomed over us like a prison. There were no lights on so the school appeared empty. The belfry tower was a long black finger that pointed up to the sky.

Straight at the Draco constellation.

Okay, now I was getting paranoid.

I squinted, trying to get a better look at the belfry. But it was too dark. I had the feeling something or someone was up there glaring down at us.

I decided not to tell Nick and Peach about this feeling.

We padded to the back of the school, moving like three ninjas in blue jeans and fall jackets. We slipped around the gym and through a maze of monkey bars and slides, then crossed the paved outdoor basketball court. Without any problem we reached the window that led to the girl's washroom.

"Okay, Nick, you boost me up," I whispered.

"Me? Why always me? Is it just because I'm the guy?" Nick could get like this sometimes.

"You're tallest. And you've got the biggest muscles," I whispered. The compliment went straight to his head.

Nick stuck his chest out and made a stirrup with his hands. "I'm ready." His voice sounded deeper.

I smiled to myself and stepped in his hand. With a

grunt and a whooshing exhalation of air, he lifted me skyward. Peach pushed from the other side, helping guide me as best as she could.

The window was closed. Obviously the janitor was doing his job a little too thoroughly. "Hold me steady," I whispered. I reached into my back pack with my right hand, unzipped the side, and pulled out a screwdriver. I jammed it into the space between the window and the sill, and when I pried it up, the window popped open.

I put my screwdriver away.

For every job there is a tool. And for every tool, there is a job. That was one of my Dad's favourite sayings.

"Hey Batgirl," Peach teased, "good thing you had the batpack on." They were always kidding me about my collection of instruments.

"Yes, it's very handy! Remember the time we had to stop that mad farmer from driving around Moose Jaw in his giant combine. Why, if I didn't have the right wrench we –"

"Hurry!" Nick wheezed.

I glanced down. His face was red and looked like a balloon about to pop.

"We'll reminisce some other time," I promised. I grabbed ahold of the sides and pulled myself through. I was pretty proud of how well I did it too. I only kicked Nick in the head once.

Next came Peach, pushing and fighting her way up to the window. You'd think she was climbing Everest. She reached the top, gave one final yank and almost took a nose dive onto the floor. I caught her at the last moment and helped her land on her feet.

Then I turned the wastebasket upside down, stood on it, reached out the window and pulled Nick up. I thought my arms would pop out of their sockets, but they held.

A moment later we were all standing on the floor, looking around. The light from the moon lit the whole room.

"So this is the girl's can," Nick said. "I always wondered what it looked like."

"Take a picture," I whispered, "'cause we're not staying long." I edged towards the door, opened it slowly, peeked out with my right eye, and looked in every direction possible. "The coast is clear," I announced. "And the hallway too."

We stepped out into the hall and headed towards the belfry, our feet as quiet as bouncing cotton balls.

Why wasn't there any squeaking, you ask. Because I was smart enough to change into my soft-soled shoes when I was home for supper. My quiet-as-a-mouse, steel-toed shoes. If you're ever doing any sneaking around, I recommend them. You could drop an anvil on your foot and it would feel like a dive-bombing fly.

Shoes are important in my business. You might say they're the very soul of it.

We crept up the stairs to the second floor, each of us looking left and right and all around. My ears grew big as radar dishes. Homing in on the slightest sound.

A clock ticked on the wall above us.

The furnace hummed below us.

And behind us...footsteps.

Heavy, clicking footsteps. And they were getting closer.

And louder.

"Quick," I whispered urgently. We ran up the steps, still quiet as mice.

We stopped at the third floor. "This way," I hissed, and we slipped through a door. Peach held it so it didn't slam.

"Who was it?" Nick asked. "Did you see?"

I shook my head. "I don't know. I hope it was one of the teachers. It had to be, right? They don't ever get enough of this place. Let's just chill here for awhile...make sure we weren't followed."

We waited. I concentrated on breathing deeply, wanting to get as much oxygen into my blood as I could. In case I had to run.

Or scream.

But no one came along, and I didn't hear anything else. So we snuck over to the door to the belfry.

It was closed. Principal Peterka had locked it.

"Here, hold this." I handed my flashlight, which I had just pulled from my backpack, to Peach. "Don't point it at me. Light up the door."

She did so. Then I dug into my pocket for a container of keys and pins, and started working on the lock.

Did I mention that my Dad was a locksmith? He runs a small store downtown. He's also my sensei – my karate instructor. In his spare time he and Mom write mystery novels together.

Anyway, it was a rather simple lock. Within a second or two I had found the right place to press and was rewarded with a:

CLICK!

Then the door creaked open. Nick and Peach clapped, very, very lightly. I put away my tools, grabbed the flashlight, and we started inside.

The stairs were as bad as last time. I showed Nick and Peach the missing step, and all three of us got over it without falling.

Up, up, up we went. The winding stairs seemed to go on forever.

Then we were in front of the belfry door at the top of the school.

I had a feeling I'd been here before: *Déjà Vu,* I think they call it in French.

I turned around, shining the light in every corner to be sure no one was behind us. Then I handed the flashlight to Peach and set to work on the belfry door.

CLICK!

I was beginning to like that sound.

I gently pushed the door open.

CHAPTER NINE

BEDLAM IN THE BELFRY

I was hit by a blast of air so cold it froze the tip of my nose and made my eyes water.

"Brrrr!" Peach whispered. "Someone crank up the heat."

She pointed the flashlight inside. Two faces appeared in the darkness, outlined in shadows and floating in the air.

"Eek!" Peach yelped. We all shuddered, then Peach directed the flashlight back at the faces.

They were masks for plays. A huge grinning one that represented comedy, and a frowning tragedy mask. They were suspended on a pole in the middle of the room.

A gallows pole.

"What is *that* doing here?" Nick asked. "Is it real?"

It was a gallows for short, short people. But it was perfectly made, even had the trapdoor for bodies to fall through. "Why is it so small?" Peach whispered.

"It's a prop," I said, the answer suddenly dawning on me. "It must have been used in a school play. Maybe this is what I saw through the keyhole."

"What kind of plays did they used to have here?" Nick moved a stick, and the trapdoor in the gallows snapped open. "Psycho plays? Or did they use that whenever someone was late with homework" He paused. "Well, at least it's not an Iron Maiden."

"Iron Maiden?" Peach asked. "Aren't they a band?"

"No," Nick said. "An Iron Maiden was a torture device made back in medieval times. It was a big casket full of spikes. They'd put the victim inside, then slowly close the door –"

"You read too many horror books," I said. "Let's get to work. Does anyone see anything weird?"

"Where's the rope?" Peach pointed at the gallows pole. "Shouldn't it be here?"

I thought for a second, my synapses working overtime. "It went out the window with Miss Vindez," I said. "They found it on her hand when she landed. She thought someone had wrapped it around her, but she might have just stumbled into it. Point the light over at the wall."

Peach pointed, lighting up a criss-crossed pattern of thick

wooden boards. "Someone blocked off the window," I said. "It was wide open this afternoon." The curtain was hanging limply on the wall. Was that what had moved? I edged closer, saw that the nails were huge. "Whoever put these boards up didn't want the window opened any time soon."

I shivered. This side of the room was somehow colder, like I'd stumbled into a freezer. A very odd environmental effect. "Let's see what else there is." I started snooping around the belfry, quietly. I picked up a small metal statue of John A. Macdonald, then set it down. My hands were smudged with decades-old dust.

Nick and Peach followed me. A big chest sat in one corner; it could have been straight from a pirate ship. Next to it were old desks, a broken broom, and stacks of dusty text books.

I reached for one that was lying open on a tiny wooden desk, picked it up. MATH it said on the front.

I set it down. Remembered something I had read only a few hours ago. "Point the light straight up."

Peach did so. At first I thought I was looking at a circular hole in the roof, surrounded by silver.

"It's the old school bell," Nick said. "It's gigantic. It looks as old as the Prime Minister."

"It's probably even older," I guessed. "Maybe more than a hundred years old. It's from a German church, originally. So I guess it's kinda holy."

We stared at it for a moment. I'd never seen a bell so large before. It was suspended in a square tower that was part of the belfry's roof. A thick rope dangled down, just out of reach.

"Wouldn't it be fun to ring it?" Nick asked. "Wouldn't that be a blast?"

"Yeah," I answered, "only if you want to spend the rest of your life in detention." I paused. "Let's see what else is here."

Peach pointed the flashlight against the far wall. There was more junk piled up, a broken globe, another heap of textbooks. We stepped towards the refuse.

There was a cracked blackboard leaning against the wall. Someone had written: 3+3= ?

And below that were the words: *I will not pull Debbie's pigtails in class.* It was written out about twenty times in neat handwriting.

"Does that mean he can pull her pigtails once they're out of class?" Nick asked.

I smiled, but kept reading. Who had written this stuff? The handwriting was right out of a textbook, with even lines and trim circles, not messy and wandering around the page like my own. "They sure could write neat in those days."

The words changed about halfway through to: *I will not close my eyes and hide my face.*

I read the line over again. What could that mean?

A piece of chalk suddenly rose up into the air. Before I could even suck in a breath, words were added to the board: *I will not be afraid of the bad man and his dirty, thick-fingered hands.*

My heart stopped beating.

The door slammed shut. I turned. "A draft blew that closed, right?" Nick asked.

The flashlight went out.

"Eeeek!" Peach screamed.

"What? What?" I reached out for her, but it was pitch black.

"Nothing," Peach said, "I was just practicing. But I do have bad news – I can't get the flashlight to come back on. It's broken."

I heard her fooling around with it. "Let me try." I reached out, found it in the darkness. No matter how hard I clicked the switch or slammed it against my other hand, it remained dead.

"I wouldn't mind a little light now," Nick whispered.

"I'm trying," I said. "It's not as easy –"

A glass broke on the far side of the room. Then came light, tinkling laughter.

Someone else was here.

My heart had kicked in again at three times its normal pace.

"What was that?" Nick asked. "Who's there?"

Something as heavy as a piano fell over behind us – scaring me so much that I dropped the flashlight. I spun around, but couldn't see through the darkness.

"Nick. Peach," I whispered. "Take my hand. Please. It sounds silly, but I want to be sure I know exactly where you are."

"It's not silly," Peach said. "It's the smartest thing I've heard tonight." I felt her warm fingers slip into my right hand.

"Yeah. It makes sense," Nick whispered. "But I don't want this to become a habit, okay? And don't tell any of the guys." His hand slipped into my left.

"Your hand's freezing," I said to him.

"So is yours. And no wonder – it's just like the Arctic in here."

Nick was right. It had gotten even colder since the door had slammed shut. It was as if someone had turned up a dial on a giant fridge. So this is what a frozen steak feels like, I thought.

"*Ring around the rosies,*" a small voice sang a few feet away.

"*Pockets full of posies,*" another voice answered from behind us.

I almost jumped out of my skin. I felt a tug on my left hand. "Don't budge," I whispered to Nick and Peach. "Whatever you do...don't even move a centimetre."

The singing had stopped, but I heard words echoing around us. I knew this song – an old one Grandma Shea used to sing to me. She had explained that the song was from the days of the black plague. The ring around the rosie was a red ring that would appear on someone's skin when they had the plague. Then people would stuff their pockets full of posies so they wouldn't smell all the dead bodies.

I was beginning to wish my grandmother hadn't taught me so much.

"*Washoo, washoo.*" This came from my left.

"*We all fall down,*" followed from my right.

This was the part of the song about people sneezing once they had the plague, then falling down dead a while later.

I was on the edge of completely freaking out.

And the weirdest thing of all was that Nick seemed to be chanting along with the song in a dry, husky voice.

Was he in a trance?

"Nick?"

"Yes," he whispered. He sounded far away.

"Why were you singing?"

"I wasn't singing. You were."

I stopped. Something had just occurred to me. "Peach. Squeeze my hand." She squeezed.

"Nick, squeeze my hand." I waited. Nothing. "Nick?"

"I squeezed it!" he whispered. "Why is it so cold?"

But my hand wasn't cold. It felt burning warm. It was his hand that was freezing. Unless.

I let go with my left hand. Took a step away.

"Nick," I whispered, trying to keep the fear out of my voice. "Am I still holding your hand?"

"Yes!" he exclaimed. "Stop fooling around. I don't like this game you're playing."

"Nick, let go!" I almost screamed it. "Let go and get over here!"

I heard a thump, then a step and suddenly a body was piling into me. "Nick! Nick! Is that you?"

"Yes! What's going on?" It *was* him. Right in front of me.

"I don't know. I think we were holding someone else's hand. Someone dead."

"What?" His voice had warbled up a few octaves.

"Just stick close, okay?" We all huddled together.

"Should we make a run for it?" Peach asked.

"Where?" I answered. "I don't even know which way the door is."

We were silent for a moment. I drew in a deep breath, trying to calm myself. It smelled like roses and flowers, like someone had opened the door to a giant garden. The air was charged with electricity.

The hairs on my arms and the back of my neck

started to stand on end.

"*Thank you for being so grand,*" a tiny voice said. "*Thank you for holding my hand.*"

CHAPTER TEN

THE BOGEYMAN

I squinted, but couldn't see anything. My throat went dry. Nick and Peach huddled closer to me.

"*No one has held my hand, I fear, for well over seventy years,*" the voice continued. Bells tinkled in the background. "*Thank you.*"

"Y-you're welcome," I whispered, my tongue dry. "Who are you?"

"*Michael Bishop,*" he said. This was followed by an explosion of tiny voices all around me that blurred into one. "*Tabitha Windthorpe. Billy Johnson. Agnes Holthorp. Teddy Dodds Timmy Ronson Betty Barbles...*"

They went on, whispering their names. I might have thought it sounded beautiful if I wasn't scared to death. Now they started to glow, tiny grey figures all around us.

I counted them. Twelve little shapes.

Michael Bishop stood so close that the buttons on his school uniform were clearly visible. There were flowers sticking out of his pocket. His sad grey eyes stared at me.

I stepped back, bumping into Nick and Peach. We backed even farther away.

Then a light bulb went on in my head. It was all starting to make sense. "You're students, aren't you? You're all dead."

"*Smoke. Fire. Hoses.*" They made a chorus. "*Pockets full of posies.*"

"You mean they're ghosts?" Nick asked. "The kids from Grudstone?" I could dimly see Nick in the glimmering light. He was pale and wide-eyed. "But the FBI Red Book said there were no such things as ghosts."

"The FBI aren't here right now, are they?" I asked. A shape floated past; I caught the smell of roses. A piece of the puzzle clicked into place. "They were all buried with flowers in their pockets. That's why we smell flowers right now."

A group of three shapes swirled like leaves in the air. "*Flee the flames, flee...everyone to the belfry.*"

Is that how they had died? Up here, smoke all around them?

"*Bad man. Big frown. Burn our whole school down.*" They were still rhyming away.

"What?" I said. "What bad man?"

"*Big man. Scary man. Had a big, bad, scary plan.*"

This is what I needed to know. "Tell me. Who was he?"

"He was an evil creature of darkness." This soft voice was not rhyming. It was Michael Bishop. "You held my hand, so I can talk normal now," he explained. He peeked over his shoulder, as if he expected a bogeyman to pop up out of nowhere. "But only for a short, short time. Hurry."

I practically spat out my question. "Who was the bad man?"

Michael shrugged his tiny grey shoulders. "Just bad. Evil. We didn't know him. Al knows his name. You ask Al."

"Al? Which one of you is Al?"

Michael shrugged again. "None of us," he said. "None of us."

"*Ring around the rosies, pocket full of posies,*" his friends chanted.

"I got to go," Michael said. "No more time. None." He sounded sad. He was starting to fade. "The Bogeyman's coming. Got to run."

"*Washooo, washooo, we all fall down.*"

Now I could hardly see him, or hear the others.

"*When the bell rings, we'll all sing and everyone will be free.*"

"Wait!" I tried to grab Michael. My hands went right through his body. "Wait."

But he was gone. They all were gone.

My flashlight flickered on. It was lying on the floor where I had dropped it, working perfectly. What kind of mystical power had stopped it from shining? I grabbed the handle and pointed the beam around.

The belfry was empty.

"They've disappeared," I said. "If they were ever really here."

We looked at each other. No one seemed to know what to say.

A key rattled in the belfry door. Hadn't Michael said the bogeyman was coming?

"Quick!" I said, grabbing one end of an old desk. "Help me!" Nick grabbed the other end, and we dragged it across the floor and jammed it against the doorknob.

The knob turned back and forth; then something thudded like a battering ram. Another booming sound followed. Someone was pounding his way in, and the thick door was going to give at any second.

"IKNOWYURINTHERE," a voice rasped, "KOMINTO-GETYOU. BADPUPILS."

"Oh no, oh no," Peach whispered. She was shaking.

"Don't worry," I said. I sounded a lot stronger than I felt. "I've got an idea. Let's get closer to the door."

"Closer? Are you nuts?" Nick asked.

"No," I whispered, walking to the door, hoping it wouldn't open. Not yet, anyway. "Whenever he – it – bursts in, we'll have to make a break for it. I'll shine my light in his eyes, blind him, then we'll run!"

"That's your plan?" Peach asked.

"We can't jump. The window's boarded up. This is the only way."

Nick and Peach stood frozen. I motioned to them, but they didn't move.

Booom!

Splinters of wood flew inward. But the desk held the door shut.

Nick and Peach scrambled to the wall behind me. We crouched by the door, waiting.

Booom! Wood snapped. The hinges almost came out of the wall. Whoever was on the other side was gigantic. "COMEOUTOFTHERE!"

Booom! And this time the door exploded inwards, knocking the desk away. A lanky figure flew into the room and turned to face us. Two gigantic eyes, glowing with madness, stared down. His hair was all wild; sweat streamed down a long, twisted face.

It was Principal Peterka. And he looked possessed and ready to tear us into confetti.

I pointed my flashlight in his eyes – he held up his

hands to block the light and made a deep groaning sound.

"Run! Run!" I yelled, dashing for the door, almost tripping over a pile of books. He grabbed at me with a hand as huge as a shovel.

I ducked underneath it, but he caught my arm and knocked the flashlight from my hand. He lifted me up and for a second I struggled, treading through the air. Then my feet found the floor.

The grips dug in.

I broke free.

Peach screamed. Loud.

Nick let out a muffled cry of anguish.

I heard some sort of struggle, a clump sound.

He had them both, one squirming under each arm.

"Run, Daphne!" Nick yelled. "Get help!"

Then I was out the door, running and running, my breathing so loud that I couldn't hear if anyone was following me.

I dashed down the spiralling stairs, leaping from step to step. The faster I went, the farther away the bottom seemed.

I heard nothing behind me.

What was he doing to Peach and Nick right now?

Down, I went. Fast as my legs would carry me. I'd get the police. I'd get my Mom and Dad. I'd call in an air strike from the Air Force base. Paratroopers would float down, their parachutes open above them. I'd get help.

How far was it to the bottom? I couldn't see anything in the dark.

I stepped into nothingness.

I had forgotten about the missing stair.

It didn't forget about me.

I fell, straight down, like a bomb.

CHAPTER ELEVEN

THE FLAPPER PRINCESS

own, down, down, I plummeted. Then I hit a wooden object feet first.

The floor.

It broke. And I dropped farther down, then bounced off a hard surface, fell another few feet and rolled on into darkness.

My trip didn't stop there. I slid, as if I was on a long waterslide. Except it was pitch black and I had no idea where I was or what was at the end of my ride. A brick wall? A pit full of spikes?

Or would there be water? With alligators?

I stuck out my arms, tried to grab the wall and slow myself down.

Too late. I was in the air. Flying. An acrobat without

a net and blind as a bat.

I crashed into something that was almost soft. Dust filled my lungs and floated all around me. It smelled like flour.

I couldn't move for a full minute. I wheezed air in and out, as if I'd never had oxygen before. My heart was beating jack rabbit fast.

I felt my face. Somehow my glasses had stayed on through all of this. Not that I could see a thing.

Where was I?

Then it all made sense. I'd fallen right through the floor at the bottom of the belfry tower and into one of the old tunnels. I was somewhere underneath Moose Jaw right now.

Way, way down.

I reached around behind me. My backpack was still there, though it felt like it had been torn in a few pieces.

I explored the pockets and found what I was looking for.

My penlight. For use in extra-special emergencies.

I figured this qualified. I clicked it on and a tiny yellow light filled the room.

I was lying on a pile of ancient flour bags with Robin Hood Mills printed in red on one side. So this is what had softened my landing. They were scattered across the floor now. If I fell again all I'd hit was rock floor. The room was small. Across from me was a slanting tunnel that led upwards. My slide.

How did I get into these messes? Why couldn't I just stay home and watch TV like most of my schoolmates? Why was I so different? Did I bump my head when I was a kid?

"Stop sulking," I told myself. "Stop it now."

You have to do that every once in awhile, give yourself a good talking to. That's what Grandma taught me and I always listened to her. Well, except for when she told me not to do anything crazy without telling her.

Hmmm. I wish I'd followed her advice.

There was no sense sitting around, though. I told myself to stand up. I stood. It didn't seem like I had broken anything, though my cheek felt sore. I must have bumped it on the way down.

I wiped the dust off my pants and shirt, then took a few steps toward the entrance.

"So you're the one who was making all the racket," a soft voice said behind me. "Are ya some kind of young flapper?"

I couldn't move. I couldn't even open my mouth. I was frozen with fright.

"I see you're kinda quiet now, aren't ya? Cat got your tongue?"

I had to do something. I didn't want to be a sitting

duck. It took all my willpower to turn around.

"Ya look a little like a flapper," he said. "Dirty though," he added. "An urchin flapper princess, maybe?"

Before me was a man dressed in a dark suit, with a silky tie and a grey businessman's hat, the kind my grandfather used to wear to church. He was thin, though his face was roundish and friendly enough. A long scar cut across his left cheek.

Oh...and he was glowing with pale, yellow-green light. Almost like he was radioactive.

He smiled. "So are ya a flapper or not?"

"Uh...I don't know." Maybe he was one of the tunnel tour guides, lost and miles from Main Street. "What's a flapper?"

"Sorry, guess it's an old word these days. I forget how much time has passed. A flapper is a woman who does whatever she wants. Dances in the streets. Says what's on her mind. Makes noise. It's the noise part that made me think you're a flapper."

"I guess I am, maybe. I don't dance much though."

He came a little closer. What was weird, though, was his feet didn't seem to move. Almost as if he was floating. I felt a chill.

"Who are ya anyway?" he asked. "Aren't you a little young for glasses? And why are ya here, kiddo? I don't get too many visitors down here."

"My name's Daphne Shea. And I just fell down here. Accidentally."

"Well, people don't usually fall down holes on purpose now, do they? Least not when I was around they didn't. Maybe things have changed, who knows?"

I stepped back a little. I was beginning to get the feeling this guy was a little nuts.

"Who are you?" I asked.

He bowed, removing his hat. He was partly bald, his head gleaming like a headlight. "Alphonso Caponi, at your service."

"Do you live down here?"

He laughed, snapped his hat back on. His teeth glittered, and I thought I saw a flash of gold inside his mouth – a golden tooth. "Live?" he echoed. "Live would be the wrong word. I dwell down here though. That would be better."

"Alphonso?" Something about his name seemed familiar. "Are you Al?" I asked, remembering what the Grudstone children had said, *Go ask Al...he knows.* There was something I was supposed to ask him.

"Yes," he said. "I'm Al. A lot of people knew me as Al. Some even called me Scarface Al, but never to my face." His jaw muscles tightened like he was remembering something bad.

Al Caponi. I ran his name through my mind a few

times. Now why did that sound so familiar? Then it hit me like a twenty ton runaway train: "You're Al Capone!" I practically yelled it. "But you...you're..."

"Dead as a doornail," he finished, smiling away. "Gone as a Thanksgiving gander. Sleeping the big sleep. Kaput! That's me. Been wandering down here for fifty some years or so. It's my punishment. And I haven't eaten a thing since the day I died." He rubbed his stomach. "You wouldn't happen to have a cracker, would you?"

"Uh...no." I stepped away from him. No wonder he was glowing.

"It doesn't matter. Everything just goes through me." He passed his own hand right through his chest and out the back. "It's my condition. Or lack of, I guess." He laughed as if he had told the funniest joke in the history of the world. He stopped, winked. "Everything's funny in the afterlife," he admitted. "So what were ya doing, running around here anyway?"

"I...I have to talk to you."

"You do?"

"Yeah. The kids. The students from Grudstone. They said you knew stuff about...about the guy who burnt down the school."

Al's face turned the color of ash. "Those kids," he whispered softly, "those poor, poor kids. I can still hear them screaming. It's partly my fault, you know."

"What happened?" I asked.

"Well, me and the gang would come up to Moose Jaw whenever we needed a vacation from the coppers – they were always following us around. So we'd lollygag around in the Jaw. We used to play cards in the school library every Sunday. We'd sneak over through the old tunnel, so the cops wouldn't have a clue where we were. We'd smoke big cigars and sit at an oak table, surrounded by books. It was the kind of room a king would love. And I'd always win. Well...the guys would let me win; they knew I'd get mad if I didn't.

"Iron Fist Ivan found out about our Sunday games. He was my enemy – well, my competition. Kind of the same thing in a way. He didn't like me hiding out in Moose Jaw – he felt it was his town. Bah! I found it first. We both liked it because you could get some good beef steaks and the coppers would never think of looking here. Also, Ivan thought it'd be a lot easier to rub me out up here while I was relaxing on vacation and my guard was down. So Ivan and several of his ugliest goons came up from Chicago. They set fire to the school, used a whole big tank of gas. We ran for our getaway tunnel. Then I heard some kids yelling. They had been practicing a play and they were cut off by the flames and couldn't get out. So they fled up to the belfry. I knew it wouldn't be safe there – I tried to get them to come down, but the flames were too high. You see, my boys had already gone ahead to make sure there were no traps in the tunnel. It was just me, yelling at these kids.

"Then Iron Fist Ivan stepped out of the shadows. He wanted to be sure he'd done the job right. And we fought. He was a big man, strong as a prize ox. And that fist of his was like a battering ram. He hit me once and nearly broke my chest in two. I skidded across the floor and he jumped at me, but I ducked. The fire was raging all around us and he had spilled a gallon of gas on himself. He landed in the flames and... well, you can probably guess what happened to him. It wasn't pretty.

"There was no way to save the kids. The fire was everywhere. I jumped in the tunnel and ran for my life.

"I guess the belfry didn't burn. No one knows why. But the kids never made it – too much smoke." He paused. "That was the last time I visited Moose Jaw. Just couldn't stand to come back here after that. Well, until I died, that is. I think it's some kind of punishment for me to haunt this tunnel. Though no one's really told me for sure."

I thought about his story. It all made sense. Except one thing. "What does this have to do with today? One of my teachers was pushed out of the belfry, and there are all these weird things going on."

Mr. Capone thought for a second. "Iron Fist Ivan was the meanest man I ever met – even meaner than me. And he wouldn't ever give up when he wanted something. He'd claw his way right back into the land of the living, if he could." He winced. "And I'm afraid he can."

"You mean he wants to be alive again?"

"More than that. He wants power. He wants control over the school. And after that, maybe Moose Jaw, who knows. At least I was happy with just Chicago. And a few parts of Moose Jaw."

"He has possession of Principal Peterka," I whispered. It all made sense now. That's why Miss Vindez had hit him and called him the filthy creature of darkness.

"The principal? That sounds right up Ivan's crooked alley." Al paused. "But he probably wants to get his old body back too."

"How does he do that?"

"Oh...there are several ways. The boys used to always tell stories about old-time pirates and thieves who came back from the other side. Something to do with matter and anti-matter transfer and saying certain words backwards. You need to get the life force or something out of a living creature – a big enough one."

"Could you use kids?"

"Kids?" He rubbed his jaw. "Yeah, kids would do. If it

was the night of Draco or some other constellation coming together."

Peach! Nick!

"I have to get back up to the school!" I exclaimed. "Two of my friends got caught by the principal. I have to go help them."

Al headed to his left. "Quickly! You can't go back the way you came. Follow me!"

He floated down a tunnel, going right through a pile of debris. I tripped over it, got up and wiped myself off. Rule number one when following a ghost – don't follow too close. I climbed over the fallen bricks and broken beams. He took a left turn, a right, went down another thin hallway. I wasn't even sure if I could find my way back.

Al stopped below an ancient ladder and pointed. "Up there. That's your ticket out."

I jogged over, grabbed the lowest rung and started upwards. I stopped a second later and turned my head to look at Al. We were almost eye to eye. "Thanks," I said. He seemed to be fading out. "You're...you're a good guy."

He shook his head. There was a look of deep sadness in his face. "No. Remember this. I wasn't good. It's not like the movies – people really bleed and suffer. I did a lot of bad things. That's why I'm down here."

I nodded. Then I turned and climbed up the ladder. At the top was a trapdoor.

I pushed it open.

CHAPTER TWELVE

THUD! KA-WUMP AND UHHHN!

I climbed up into darkness and slowly lowered the trap-door.

I was standing in the middle of a pitch black room that had a familiar dusty, warm smell. I sniffed. I couldn't see a thing, but I knew the room. Or I should know it. I sniffed again.

I'd smelled this smell a million times.

It was the scent of old books and new magazines. I was standing in my favourite room in the whole school – the library.

I wondered if I should risk using my penlight, then realized the brightness might show Principal Peterka my position. I decided to feel my way around.

I squinted. The pale moon shone through the

windows high in the wall. I made out the shapes of shelves and large, thick books. As far as I could tell I was in the back of the library, in the science section.

My eyes adjusted even more. I saw the outline of book racks and tables – but not much else. I'd have to remember to ask Mom and Dad for some night vision goggles for Christmas, and a periscope so I could peer around corners.

"Do the best with what you have," Grandma always told me. So I put my arms out in front of me like a sleep-walker and began edging towards the door. I took little baby steps, so I wouldn't kick anything over or trip.

With each step I realized I was able to see better. Almost as if the room was getting brighter.

Then it dawned on me: it *was* getting brighter. A flickering light was just on the other side of a tall book-shelf, casting shadows on the walls. I turned a corner and saw a confused mess of candles burning along the far wall of the library. There was a small mannequin hanging on the wall.

I stepped to my left, past a row of books, then another. I headed down an aisle, and when I got to the end I could view everything clearer.

There wasn't one mannequin, but two. They looked kind of like the straw men you see out in gardens with their heads hanging down. There were candles set all around on shelves and piles of books, burning brightly and dripping wax.

What the heck was going on?

I took a few more quiet steps.

One of the mannequins moved.

I stared, eyes wide open.

They weren't straw men or mannequins. They were people. Two kids I knew really well.

Peach and Nick! Someone had hung them on the wall like oversized Christmas decorations. Little metal electrodes were connected to their skulls, lines leading down and hooked into a car battery. A suction tube ran above them and down to the school's portable vacuum. Several beakers sat around, bubbling a harsh-smelling pink substance. It looked like a science class run by Dr. Frankenstein.

I glanced left and right, for their abductor. Principal Peterka had to be here somewhere. All the candles and scientific instruments must be for some sort of experiment.

An experiment to bring Iron Fist Ivan back from the dead.

One of the candles was at the top of the bookshelf, up near the clock. It was ten minutes to twelve.

And midnight was the witching hour.

I had to do something and do it quick.

I moved over to my left, hiding behind bookshelves. I didn't want to walk straight up to them in case it was some sort of a trap. I listened for the slightest noise, then crab-walked forward, slowly and quietly. My knees ached, but I carried on, getting closer and closer.

Someone grabbed me out of the dark and pulled me to the floor. A rough, callused hand covered my mouth.

"Don't struggle," a male voice hissed in my ear.

I didn't move. My eyes grew as wide as saucers.

"It's me," he said. "Don't scream." He sounded more friendly. He pulled his hand away from my mouth.

"Me who?" I whispered.

"Mr. Eckerweir, the janitor, at your service."

I breathed in a sigh of relief. "Mr. Eckerweir."

"My head is clear now," he said. "Principal Peterka is doing bad things. First I saw him making strange faces in the mirror as if it was the first time he'd ever used his face. Then when I was cleaning his office I found a book called *101 Ways to Bring Back the Dead*. And he was talking to himself. I think it was him who bound me up behind the incinerator."

"Where is he now?" I asked.

"He left the room a few minutes ago. To get something for his experiment. We don't have much time. We have to help those two kids, Sandra and Steve."

"Nick and Peach," I corrected him.

"Right...I'm sorry, I get you kids mixed up all the time. You all move so fast." He rose. "I want you to distract him and I'll give him a knock on the bean. Okay?"

"Uh. Sounds like a good plan."

I tagged along behind him. We moved carefully up to the candles and into the circle of light. Nick was struggling a little; he seemed to be waking up. Peach was out like a light.

They both had gags on. Mr. Eckerweir went to the left, I wasn't sure why. I stepped ahead until I was only a few feet away from my friends. They were tied with ropes. The knots were thick and tight, obviously done by an expert.

Nick opened his eyes as wide as could be. He started gnashing his teeth as if he wanted to say something. His face was pale with fright.

"It's okay," I whispered in my most soothing voice. "I'll have you untied in a jiffy. Soon we'll be sitting at home, eating gingersnaps and laughing about this."

Nick motioned with his head. His eyes were so big now I thought they'd pop right out.

Then I saw Principal Peterka out of the corner of my eye.

He was leaping for me, yelling, "Daphne! Watch –"

Eckerweir jumped up from behind a bookshelf and swung a fire extinguisher, hitting his target perfectly: *thud!*

With a *ka-wump* Principal Peterka fell to the floor. He said "*Uhhn*" once, then lay motionless, eyes closed. I leaned a little closer. Principle Peterka was out cold, sprawled across the hardwood.

"You did it!" I said. "You got him! Now all we have to do is get him unpossessed."

Before I could turn to shake Mr. Eckerweir's hand I was grabbed from behind, by hands that squeezed like giant vice grips. My arms were pinned to my side, then pulled back. A second later I was hog-tied and spun around.

Mr. Eckerweir was grinning like a maniac.

CHAPTER THIRTEEN

PSYCHO JANITOR

"HA HA HA HA HA HA HA!" He laughed for about thirty seconds straight, his bald head bobbing up and down like a pink bowling ball. "HA HA HA HA HA HA!"

"Mr. Eckerweir?" I shouted. "Are you alright? Let me go!"

"Daffy Daphne," he said. "You silly little flapper of a girl. Don't you get it? It was me all along."

"No one calls me Daffy Daphne," I said, quietly.

"I do. In a few minutes I'm going to be in complete control of everything in this school. The stars are right, the time is now. I shall live again. HA HA HA!" He threw his head back once more. He seemed to like laughing.

And then it all made sense. I could be a little slow

sometimes. "You're Iron Fist Ivan, aren't you? Give up, go back to where you came from, give us our janitor back."

He guffawed. I say guffawed because it wasn't laughing, it was a deep, loud, rumbling sound. "I've never been so bored," he said, "hanging around the school all this time since the fire. Watching them build a new one, watching the kids file in and file out, year after year. Then, at last, the moment was right for me to strike."

"I found your poor janitor in the janitor's room, snoozing away, his head resting against his mop. He watches a lot o' those soaps. Weakens the mind, makes it easier to take over. Poor unsuspecting sucker – he didn't know what hit him. First he thought it was a bad daydream. Then, next thing he knew, I had control of his shrimpy little body. Yeah, I know, he's knee high to a grasshopper – I wish I'd gotten control of someone bigger, but it was a good start."

He paused long enough for me to interject: "You taped yourself up and hid by the incinerator. Just to get me off your trail."

"Clever, aren't I?"

There was one question that had to be answered. "But if it was you all along, why did Miss Vindez hit the principal?"

He laughed again – I was getting sick of the sound. "That's the funny part. She was trying to hit me, to warn everyone about me, but just then the principal leaned in to see how she was, and POW, she almost knocked him right out of his shoes. You should've seen the look on his face. Served the snoop right."

Ivan pointed at Principal Peterka. "That's what sleeping beauty was doing tonight, snooping around the school. I think he knew something was going on, but he couldn't figure out what. He captured your two friends for me, then locked them up in his office while he went to find you. I slipped in, slipped out with them and set all this up. I was hoping to have my little experiment finished before he came back, but then you showed up. Perfect timing!"

I was beginning to realize this Iron Fist Ivan liked to talk. A lot. Maybe I could use it to my advantage by keeping him blabbing while I loosened my knots. "But why are you doing all this?" I asked.

"Why?" he grinned at me, his eyes large and glowing with humor. "Why? How would you like to spend your time wandering through the halls of a school every night? Year after year after boring year?" He paused. "But that's not the real reason. Ever since I was born I liked pulling wings off flies and pushing people into puddles. It's because I'm bad, that's why. I don't need any other reasons. You really are a little Daffy."

"Don't say that," I warned. I wasn't scared any more.

Something moved in a corner of the library. A grey shape. A second one floated into view. Then I heard soft gentle singing:

"*Ring around the rosie,*
Pocket full of posies."

It was the children from the belfry. They had somehow wandered down here.

Iron Fist Ivan hadn't noticed them yet. "I'm going to take this town to the cleaners. Moose Jaw will never know what hit it. It's gonna be like the good ol' days. I'm going to make the headlines in all the papers! Iron Fist Ivan, King of crime and ruler of Moose Jaw. I'm going to...eh?" He stopped. "What's that?"

More of the ghostly students were flooding in, coming through the walls, drifting around.

"Well, if it isn't the brats from the belfry," he said, "The stars are right – I guess that means a few kiddie ghosts can wander too." He grabbed a candle. "You guys still scared of fire?"

He pushed the candle close to one of the grey shapes. It shrieked and flitted away, moaning, "*Flame, flame, never touch me again.*"

"Ha Ha Ha," Iron Fist Ivan laughed. "You kids never were too smart."

All this time I'd been working the knots on my wrists. I recognized the loops; it was *The Spider's Belly*. My Grandma had taught me all about it. The tighter you pulled, the tighter it got. I relaxed my hands and found the right place to tug and loosen it.

Ivan was wielding the candle like a sword, frightening the ghosts. He laughed, then turned to me. "Silly kids," he said, "HA HA!" He poked the flame towards another shape and it scooted away. Ivan set the candle down. "They tried to save that silly Miss Vindez who was out snooping in the belfry. Tried to warn her, but too late. I tossed the biddy out a window. That's *my* belfry. No one's supposed to go in there. Too many secret things from the past in there."

The ghosts were still drifting around in the distant part of the library, singing:

"Ding dong, dang, ding.
Dong, ding, dang, dong."

What were they doing here? If this was their first time out of the belfry, why would they go anywhere near the man who had started the fire in their school?

"It's almost time," Ivan said. "Even the kid ghosts are a sign that it's getting close." He glanced at the clock. "Now," he said, "let's begin the experiment."

He pulled on a book high on a shelf. "Watch carefully, Daphne."

Part of the wall started to move. "You maybe didn't know it, but the library and the belfry are all that's left of the old school. This is one of the secret compartments." A section of books turned around like a revolving door.

On the other side was a coffin. All dusty and about eight feet long.

"It's my body," Ivan explained as he plugged several electrodes into the side of the coffin. "My boys brought it here for me. I haunted them until they dug it up, cause I knew one day I'd be able to get back into it again. I can dump this shrimpy janitor's body. In a minute, now." His old body had been sitting there for over seventy years. Waiting in a coffin. I didn't want to see it. I didn't want to imagine what it would look like now. Or smell like.

Ivan stuck several electrodes onto my forehead, using the pink goo from the beakers. I tried to move my head out of the way, but failed.

"You look worried, Daphne. Don't be. When the clock strikes twelve the electrodes will sparkle with electricity, and begin jostling your life force. Then I'll hit the switch on the vacuum and the life force will be sucked out of you and your friends and shot into the coffin, bringing my ol' body back to life. Simple, eh? You won't feel a thing."

The grey ghostly kids were still floating around, seemed to be moving faster.

"Ding dong, won't be round too long,
Ding dong, ring the bell today."

"It's twelve. Time to flick the switch." He turned and leaned over the car battery. A light switch was attached to it by two wires.

My heart started to race. I worked at the knot, but I wasn't relaxed enough. It just tightened against my wrists.

"Ivan!" a deep voice called, so deep the whole library shook like an earthquake. "Iron Fist Ivan!"

Ivan turned around. "Who is it?" he asked.

Suddenly a head floated towards us in mid-air. It was wearing a hat. Then the body appeared in a suit.

It was Al Capone, smiling and thin, his fists held out in a boxer's pose.

"Scarface," Ivan said, "I knew you were still lurking around. I could smell you."

"I'm taking you down, Ivan," Al promised, and with that he flew across the room.

"A ghost could never touch me," Ivan said, hands on his hips. "You have no physical form."

Al hit him, knocking Ivan to the ground. "Hey.

What's going on?" Ivan shouted.

"It's witching hour and Draco's rising, so for a few minutes I can throw some punches. It's time to put you in the hurt locker."

Ivan grabbed Al in a bear hug and they struggled with each other, knocking over a bookshelf. A glass beaker fell to the floor, smashing and releasing a red cloud of fumes.

Three of the ghost kids were suddenly in front of me, singing in urgent tones, *The bells go up. The bells go down. And the bad man goes into the ground.*

What did that mean?

Suddenly, I knew why they were here. They were trying to tell me something.

I pulled on the knot. The ropes fell.

I stripped the electrodes off and ran for the library door. Past Iron Fist Ivan who was struggling with the ghost of Al Capone. He seemed to be winning – using his fist to drive Al back down into the floor, as if he were hammering in a nail.

I dashed for the door.

Behind me I heard a scream.

"DAPHNE!!!" Ivan yelled. "DAPHNE!"

But I was out of the library doors and running razzle dazzle for the belfry. Grey shapes flitted past me, guiding me ahead. I pounded my feet, urging my knees to pump faster.

A door banged open behind me. Ivan was right on my tail.

I sprinted up the stairs to the third floor. Then I was through the door and taking the steps to the belfry two or three at a time, wishing my legs would grow longer. Somehow I jumped the missing stair. I tripped once, pulled myself up and headed onwards.

Ivan was pounding his way up the stairs so loud it sounded like he was breaking every step. I hoped he'd fall right through.

I got to the top and came to the door. It was closed and locked. Some of the boards were broken from the Principal's battering, but I couldn't push my way through.

I grabbed the knob and twisted it back and forth.

Ivan was gaining on me every second. His steps echoed like sonic booms. "DAPHNEEEEEE!" he screamed, and I wondered if he wasn't changing into some sort of beast. "DAPHNEEEEEEEEE!"

The ghosts were flitting around me again, giving off enough pale light that I could see the keyhole. I dug in my pockets for my lock picks, found them and set to work. My fingers sweated. The pick slipped. Then I shoved it in again and *click*.

The door opened. I pushed and jumped inside. A hand grabbed my leg, and I fell headlong into the belfry.

"STOP RIGHT THERE!" Ivan screamed. He was standing above me. I kicked at him and broke free. "I WILL CURSE YOU FOREVER IF YOU DON'T STOP THERE!"

He leaped at me, grabbed, but I twisted out of the way. The ghosts flitted around like giant grey fireflies. The janitor's face was all twisted and distorted, like a reflection in a carnival mirror. He was so mad he was slobbering.

He grabbed my shoulder. I turned and kicked him, aiming for his shin.

I hit higher. Between his legs. I know you're never supposed to ever kick anyone there. Unless you're in a belfry and fighting to save your life and your friends and your school too.

He doubled over and released me.

"That was for Miss Vindez," I said.

Then I turned away from him, climbed the scaffold, and grabbed the rope to the bell, the school bell that had done nothing but collect dust for decades. It was a thick old rotting rope.

Nothing happened. I tugged again. Nothing.

Then I swung as far as I could and swooshed through the air, a tight grip on the rope.

The bell rang.

For the first time in over seventy years.

DING DONG DING DONG

Calling all the students. Waves of sound echoing through the room, the school, and across all of Moose Jaw.

Magic reverberations. From a school bell. A church bell.

At midnight, the witching hour.

When anything could happen.

Grey shadows flitted past my eyes, jittered around, then slowed.

I kept ringing the bell.

DING DONG DING DONG DING DONG

The shapes took form, became the kids from the class of '27 assembled in front of me. Looking a lot like they did in the picture from that old book.

"The bell is rung, our time is done,
bless you, bless you, our song is sung."

I dropped to the floor and wiped off my hands. The bell kept ringing.

The students were smiling, the magic notes going through them. For a second I saw them clearly, saw what they were like when they were kids. Young and happy. Smiling. And laughing.

They bowed.

Then, one by one, they disappeared, flicking off like

lights that someone had extinguished. Till I was alone.

And still the final echo of the bell hadn't stopped. That final DONG would reverberate forever.

It took me a moment to find my penlight and click it on. Mr. Eckerweir was passed out, draped across the floor. I hesitantly approached. He didn't move, except to lightly snore. I lifted up his eyelids, shone the light in his eyes. They looked normal. A little bloodshot, but not possessed. I wiped my forehead with the back of my hand, and a sudden sense of relief passed through me.

I would need help to get him out of here. I saw my other flashlight near the door, where Principal Peterka had knocked it from my hands earlier in the evening. When I picked it up, it worked perfectly.

I went down the stairs slowly, planning to free Nick and Peach. Every bone ached, but I felt fine. I was so glad that it had worked out. Somehow I had stopped it all.

I almost fell down the missing stair, but caught myself and stepped over it. Soon I was at the bottom.

There was a noise like something wet and heavy moving across the floor, moving so quickly that I couldn't turn in time to see it.

A cold, clammy hand grabbed me.

CHAPTER FOURTEEN

STOMPIN' WHITE WORMS

I was spun around.

A man stood in front of me, about three times my height, clad in a rotted suit, his skin burned and lumpy. He leaned lopsidedly, his hair had fallen out in clumps, his eyes were glowing the colour of the moon. His right fist was made of rusted metal.

Iron Fist Ivan. In his old body.

Somehow I had failed.

"DAAAAAPHNEEE," he snarled out of one side of his thick-lipped mouth. "CRUSSSSSSH YOU."

He squeezed his left hand tighter on my shoulder and picked me up.

I fought to free myself, but he was a hundred times stronger than me.

"DAAAAAAAPHNNEEEEEE." His breath stank like a garburator stuffed with orange peels, rotten apples and crushed cantaloupe a hundred years old. When he brought up his iron fist, the rusted metal knuckles hypnotized me. He shook me like a piñata. "CRUSHHHH YOU."

He squeezed, but his hand was slippery with goo. I slid out of his grip and fell to the floor. I scrambled to my feet, but he was right there, blocking the only way out. I backed away from him.

He lumbered ahead. One slow plodding step after another.

I was cornered.

I stepped back a little farther, felt a ledge.

I was on the edge of the broken trapdoor to the underground tunnel. I could slide down there, I thought, then run.

But he would follow me. And I'd be caught underground.

So I turned and took a small step towards him. He paused, confused by this. Then I spun again and with a hop and a step I jumped over the gaping hole.

But not far enough.

I caught the ledge with my hands, clung to it with all my strength. For a moment my feet dangled in mid-air. Then with an effort that I can only call gigantomungus, I yanked myself up.

I balanced on the ledge.

Iron Fist Ivan stood ten feet away from me, the pit between us. His eyes glowed. His mouth opened and closed like an animal's. "DAPHNEEEEE."

"Come and get me, you big, ugly doofus," I said.

He gave me a shocked look.

"Yeah, you heard me," I yelled. "You're a googly-eyed, second-rate gangster."

He growled. His nostrils flared.

"Yeah, come on," I continued, "or are you chicken? Bock. Bock –"

He crouched, then released like a giant spring. He shot through the air, coming straight towards me as big as a rhino, reaching out, ready to crush me.

Then he fell into the pit.

Except his left hand latched onto the ledge. He hung there, growling and hissing and spitting. He tried to use his iron fist to grab on, but it broke the wood. He was right below me.

"Guess that iron fist isn't so handy now, is it?" I asked.

Enraged by my taunt, he started to pull himself up with one hand, eyes glowing red now.

There was no place for me to go. I couldn't jump over him. I couldn't back any farther into the wall.

So I did the only think I could think of:

I stomped on one of his fingers.

He screamed. I stomped on the next one.

Then I heard a *whooshing whishing* sound, and there was Al Capone, wrapped around Ivan's legs, trying to pull him down into the tunnel.

I stomped again. Ivan lifted a finger, still screaming.

It was like squashing giant worms. I stomped again.

He was clinging by just one thick index finger. He opened his mouth to snarl once more.

"No one calls me Daffy Daphne," I shouted. Then I landed on his finger with both feet.

He screamed. Let go. And fell, banging against the sides of the slide, down into the tunnels below Moose Jaw, his voice echoing up to me.

There was a giant thud, the sound of a huge sack of potatoes hitting cement.

And nothing. No noise. Not a word. Not a sound.

I couldn't see a thing.

I quietly shuffled my way along the edge and over to the side. Then stepped away from the broken trapdoor.

A ghostly head popped out of the floor beside me. It was wearing a hat.

"He's dead as a dodo," Al said, smiling. "He kinda fell to pieces on his way down. It's really not very pretty." He pinched his nose. "Smells a little too."

I held my stomach.

"Bye bye to bad rubbish, is what I say." Al winked. "I

gotta go. I think my time is done. I hear voices calling me. Ever since that bell rang."

He was starting to glimmer. And to fade. "What kind of voices?"

"It's my Mom," he answered. "She's calling me to supper. I finally get to eat."

Then he vanished into thin air with a popping sound. There was a smell of sulfur, like someone had just struck a match.

I didn't even get to say goodbye, I realized.

I took a step.

Al appeared again, a piece of chicken in his hand. "You have no idea how good this grub tastes." He chewed for a second, took another bite and spoke. "Just one more thing," he said. "I wanted to say you're a darn fine young flapper. And I'd work with you again, any time." He winked. Put his hand to his ear. "There's my mom again. I guess the rest of supper's ready. And there's apple pie too. It's been wonderful. Goodbye."

"Goodbye," I answered.

He was gone. Maybe forever.

I stood there for a moment. Feeling sad.

Then I remembered Nick and Peach.

CHAPTER FIFTEEN

ALL'S WELL THAT ENDS WELL ...KIND OF

I ran to the library.

My two best friends in the whole world were still hanging from the wall, struggling to get off. When they saw me, they stopped and sighed. I dashed up and untied them as fast as I could. Once I got them loose, they stood rubbing their hands.

"What happened?" Nick asked. "All I remember is Eckerweir laughing and the sound of a vacuum. It felt like my brains were being sucked out."

Peach patted her head. "Hey, who messed up my hair!" She pulled away her hand; a pink glob was stuck to it. "And what's this stuff?"

"It's some kind of ectoplasm," I explained. "Ghost goo. We were all part of an experiment to bring back Iron Fist Ivan from the dead."

"The gangster from Chicago!" Nick exclaimed. "Back from the dead? But... But..." For the first time in his life he was lost for words.

"What happened, Daphne?" Peach asked.

"It's simple, really," I began. "We should have seen it right from the start. The first clue was..."

Principal Peterka suddenly sat up, pressed his hand against his head. "Owwwch!" he moaned. I helped him stand. He blinked a few times, his eyes focusing on me. "You! You are in detention forever, as far as I'm concerned. You and your two friends." He looked at all the candles and leftovers from the science room. "What is this mess? What were you doing? Explain this to me right now, Daphne Shea."

All three of them stared at me.

"Well," I said, after a long and probably dramatic pause, "I don't think you'd even believe me if I told you. It has to do with Grudstone School, Al Capone and ghosts."

"Miss Shea," he said, still rubbing his head. "If this is some kind of joke, it's not funny."

"It's not a joke," a voice said from the doorway.

Grandma Shea was standing there in her track suit.

"I heard the belfry bell. It hasn't rung in my lifetime. I knew something was going on. And that it would have something to do with my granddaughter." She paused, gave me an sharp look. "Didn't I tell you to call me first?"

"Uh," I said slowly, stalling for time, "Uh...let me explain. It will take a while, and I do have a few things to show all of you. I know how angry you must be, Mr. Peterka, and you have every right to be angry. But I would never break a school rule unless I absolutely had to. Will you listen to my story? I know Grandma will back me up."

When Principal Peterka looked at Grandma, she nodded. "Fine," he said, "explain away."

"First we should get Mr. Eckerweir from the belfry; then all of us can head down to the lunch room for some hot chocolate. I'll start the story right at the very beginning."

They all nodded and we left the library.

And that's how my adventure with the Grudstone ghosts ended. Pretty crazy stuff, eh?

Someday I'll tell you what happened during the second week of school.

ACKNOWLEDGEMENTS

I wish to thank Bob Currie for his help with this story and extend my gratitude to the people of Moose Jaw. I was born there and spent many a happy weekend visiting the city. Therefore, it seemed natural to write a "haunted" story as a thank you.

ABOUT THE AUTHOR

Arthur Slade is the author of *Dust*, which won the Governor General's Award for Children's Literature in 2001. His other titles include *Draugr*, *The Haunting of Drang Island*, *The Loki Wolf*, and *Tribes*. Raised on a ranch in Saskatchewan's Cypress Hills, he now lives in Saskatoon.